# The Spanish

Maurice Hewlett

**Alpha Editions**

This edition published in 2024

ISBN : 9789361476846

Design and Setting By
**Alpha Editions**
www.alphaedis.com
Email - info@alphaedis.com

# Contents

# INTRODUCTION

Cada puta hile (Let every jade go spin).—SANCHO PANZA.

Almost alone in Europe stands Spain, the country of things as they are. The Spaniard weaves no glamour about facts, apologises for nothing, extenuates nothing. *Lo que ha de ser no puede faltar!* If you must have an explanation, here it is. Chew it, Englishman, and be content; you will get no other. One result of this is that Circumstance, left naked, is to be seen more often a strong than a pretty thing; and another that the Englishman, inveterately a draper, is often horrified and occasionally heart-broken. The Spaniard may regret, but cannot mend the organ. His own will never suffer the same fate. *Chercher le midi à quatorze heures* is no foible of his.

The state of things cannot last; for the sentimental pour into the country now, and insist that the natives shall become as self-conscious as themselves. The *Sud-Express* brings them from England and Germany, vast ships convey them from New York. Then there are the newspapers, eager as ever to make bricks without straw. Against Teutonic travellers, and journalists, no idiosyncrasy can stand out. The country will run to pulp, as a pear, bitten without by wasps and within by a maggot, will get sleepy and drop. But that end is not yet, the Lord be praised, and will not be in your time or mine. The tale I have to tell—an old one, as we reckon news now—might have happened yesterday; for that was when I was last in Spain, and satisfied myself that all the concomitants were still in being. I can assure you that many a Don Luis yet, bitterly poor and bitterly proud, starves and shivers, and hugs up his bones in his *capa* between the Bidassoa and the Manzanares; many a wild-hearted, unlettered Manuela applies the inexorable law of the land to her own detriment, and, with a sob in the breath, sits down to her spinning again, her mouldy crust and cup of cold water, or worse fare than that. Joy is not for the poor, she says—and then, with a shrug, *Lo que ha de ser...!*

But, as a matter of fact, it belongs to George Borrow's day, this tale, when gentlemen rode a-horseback between town and town, and followed the river-bed rather than the road. A stranger then, in the plains of Castile, was either a fool who knew not when he was well off, or an unfortunate, whose misery at home forced him afield. There was no *genus* Tourist; the traveller was conspicuous and could be traced from Spain to Spain. When you get on you'll see; that is how Tormillo weaselled out Mr. Manvers, by the smell of his blood. A great, roomy, haggard country, half desert waste and half bare rock, was the Spain of 1860, immemorially old, immutably the same, splendidly frank, acquainted with grief and sin, shameless and free;

like some brown gipsy wench of the wayside, with throat and half her bosom bare, who would laugh and show her teeth, and be free with her jest; but if you touched her honour, ignorant that she had one, would stab you without ruth, and go her free way, leaving you carrion in the ditch. Such was the Spain which Mr. Manvers visited some fifty years ago.

# CHAPTER I

## THE PLEASANT ERRAND

Into the plain beyond Burgos, through the sunless glare of before-dawn; upon a soft-padding ass that cast no shadow and made no sound; well upon the stern of that ass, and with two bare heels to kick him; alone in the immensity of Castile, and as happy as a king may be, rode a young man on a May morning, singing to himself a wailing, winding chant in the minor which, as it had no end, may well have had no beginning. He only paused in it to look before him between his donkey's ears; and then—"*Arré, burra, hijo de perra!*"—he would drive his heels into the animal's rump. In a few minutes the song went spearing aloft again .... "*En batalla-a-a temero-o-sa-a....!*"

I say that he was young; he was very young, and looked very delicate, with his transparent, alabaster skin, lustrous grey eyes and pale, thin lips. He had a sagging straw hat upon his round and shapely head, a shirt—and a dirty shirt—open to the waist. His *faja* was a broad band of scarlet cloth wound half a dozen times about his middle, and supported a murderous long knife. For the rest, cotton drawers, bare legs, and feet as brown as walnuts. All of him that was not whitey-brown cotton or red cloth was the colour of the country; but his cropped head was black, and his eyes were very light grey, keen, restless and bold. He was sharp-featured, careless and impudent; but when he smiled you might think him bewitching. His name he would give you as Estéban Vincaz—which it was not; his affair was pressing, pleasant and pious. Of that he had no doubt at all. He was intending the murder of a young woman.

His eyes, as he sang, roamed the sun-struck land, and saw everything as it should be. Life was a grim business for man and beast and herb of the field, no better for one than for the others. The winter corn in patches struggled sparsely through the clods; darnels, tares, deadnettle and couch, the vetches of last year and the thistles of next, contended with it, not in vain. The olives were not yet in flower, but the plums and sloes were powdered with white; all was in order.

When a clump of smoky-blue iris caught his downward looks, he slipped off his ass and snatched a handful for his hat. "The Sword-flower," he called it, and accepting the omen with a chuckle, jumped into his seat again and kicked the beast with his naked heels into the shamble that does duty for a pace. As he decorated his hat-string he resumed his song:—

"En batalla temerosa
Andaba el Cid castellano
Con Búcar, ese rey moro,
Que contra el Cid ha llegado
A le ganar a Valencia..."

He hung upon the pounding assonances, and his heart thumped in accord, as if his present adventure had been that crowning one of the hero's.

Accept him for what he was, the graceless son of his parents—horse-thief, sheep-thief, contrabandist, bully, trader of women—he had the look of a seraph when he sang, the complacency of an angel of the Weighing of Souls. And why not? He had no doubts; he could justify every hour of his life. If money failed him, wits did not; he had the manners of a gentleman—and a gentleman he actually was, hidalgo by birth—and the morals of a hyaena, that is to say, none at all. I doubt if he had anything worth having except the grand air; the rest had been discarded as of no account.

Schooling had been his, he had let it slip; if his gentlehood had been negotiable he had carded it away. Nowadays he knew only elementary things—hunger, thirst, fatigue, desire, hatred, fear. What he craved, that he took, if he could. He feared the dark, and God in the Sacrament. He pitied nothing, regretted nothing; for to pity a thing you must respect it, and to respect you must fear; and as for regret, when it came to feeling the loss of a thing it came naturally also to hating the cause of its loss; and so the greater lust swallowed up the less.

He had felt regret when Manuela ran away; it had hurt him, and he hated her for it. That was why he intended at all cost to find her again, and to kill her; because she had been his *amiga*, and had left him. Three weeks ago, it had been, at the fair of Pobledo. The fair had been spoiled for him, he had earned nothing, and lost much; esteem, to wit, his own esteem, mortally wounded by the loss of Manuela, whose beauty had been a mark, and its possession an asset; and time—valuable time—lost in finding out where she had gone.

Friends of his had helped him; he had hailed every *arriero* on the road, from Pamplona to La Coruña; and when he had what he wanted he had only delayed for one day, to get his knife ground. He knew exactly where she was, at what hour he should find her, and with whom. His tongue itched and brought water into his mouth when he pictured the meeting. He pictured it now, as he jogged and sang and looked contentedly at the endless plain.

Presently he came within sight, and, since he made no effort to avoid it, presently again into the street of a mud-built village. Few people were astir. A man slept in an angle of a wall, flies about his head; a dog in an entry scratched himself with ecstasy; a woman at a doorway was combing her child's hair, and looked up to watch him coming.

Entering in his easy way, he looked to the east to judge of the light. Sunrise was nearly an hour away; he could afford to obey the summons of the cracked bell, filling the place with its wrangling, with the creaking of its wheel. He hobbled his beast in the little *plaza*, and followed some straying women into church.

Immediately confronting him at the door was a hideous idol. A huge and brown, wooden Christ, with black horse-hair tresses, staring white eyeballs, staring red wounds, towered before him, hanging from a cross. Estéban knelt to it on one knee, and, remembering his hat, doffed it sideways over his ear. He said his two *Paternosters*, and then performed one odd ceremony more. Several people saw him do it, but no one was surprised. He took the long knife from his *faja*, running his finger lightly along the edge, laid it flat before the Cross, and looking up at the tormented God, said him another *Pater*. That done, he went into the church, and knelt upon the floor in company with kerchiefed women, children, a dog or two, and some beggars of incredible age and infirmities beyond description, and rose to one knee, fell to both, covered his eyes, watched the celebrant, or the youngest of the women, just as the server's little bell bade him. Simple ceremonies, done by rote and common to Latin Europe; certainly not learned of the Moors.

Mass over, our young avenger prepared to resume his journey by breaking his fast. A hunch of bread and a few raisins sufficed him, and he ate these sitting on the steps of the church, watching the women as they loitered on their way home. Estéban had a keen eye for women; pence only, I mean the lack of them, prevented him from being a collector. But the eye is free; he viewed them all from the standpoint of the cabinet. One he approved. She carried herself well, had fine ankles, and wore a flower in her hair like an Andalusian. Now, it was one of his many grudges against fate that he had never been in Andalusia and seen the women there. For certain, they were handsome; a *Sevillana*, for instance! Would they wear flowers in their hair—over the ear—unless they dared be looked at? Manuela was of Valencia, more than half *gitana*: a wonderfully supple girl. When she danced the *jota* it was like nothing so much as a snake in an agony. Her hair was tawny yellow, and very long. She wore no flower in it, but bound a red handkerchief in and out of the plaits. She was vain of her hair—heart of God, how he hated her!

Then the priest came out of church, fat, dewlapped, greasy, very short of breath, but benevolent. "Good-day, good-day to you," he said. "You are a stranger. From the North?"

"My reverence, from Burgos."

"Ha, from Burgos this morning! A fine city, a great city."

"Yes, sir, it's true. It is where they buried our lord the Campeador."

"So they say. You are lettered! And early afoot."

"Yes, sir. I am called to be early. I still go South."

"Seeking work, no doubt. You are honest, I hope?"

"Yes, sir, a very honest Christian. But I seek no work. I find it."

"You are lucky," said the priest, and took snuff. "And where is your work? In Valladolid, perhaps?"

Estéban blinked hard at that last question. "No, sir," he said. "Not there." Do what he might he could not repress the bitter gleam in his eyes.

The old priest paused, his fingers once more in the snuff-box. "There again you have a great city. Ah, and there was a time when Valladolid was one of the greatest in Castile. The capital of a kingdom! Chosen seat of a king! Pattern of the true Faith!" His eyelids narrowed quickly. "You do not know it?"

"No, sir," said Estéban gently. "I have never been there."

The priest shrugged. "*Vaya*! it is no affair of mine," he said. Then he waved his hand, wagging it about like a fan. "Go your ways," he added, "with God."

"Always at the feet of your reverence," said Estéban, and watched him depart. He stared after him, and looked sick.

Altogether he delayed for an hour and a quarter in this village: a material time. The sun was up as he left it—a burning globe, just above the limits of the plain.

# CHAPTER II

## THE TRAVELLER AT LARGE

Ahead of Estéban some five or six hours, or, rather converging upon a common centre so far removed from him, was one Osmund Manvers, a young English gentleman of easy fortune, independent habits and analytical disposition; also riding, also singing to himself, equally early afoot, but in very different circumstances. He bestrode a horse tolerably sound, had a haversack before him reasonably stored. He had a clean shirt on him, and another embaled, a brace of pistols, a New Testament and a "Don Quixote"; he wore brown knee-boots, a tweed jacket, white duck breeches, and a straw hat as little picturesque as it was comfortable or convenient. Neither revenge nor enemy lay ahead, of him; he travelled for his pleasure, and so pleasantly that even Time was his friend. Health was the salt of his daily fare, and curiosity gave him appetite for every minute of the day.

He would have looked incongruous in the elfin landscape—in that empty plain, under that ringing sky—if he had not appeared to be as extremely at home in it as young Estéban himself; but there was this farther difference to be noted, that whereas Estéban seemed to belong to the land, the land seemed to belong to Mr. Manvers—the land of the Spains and all those vast distances of it, the enormous space of ground, the dim blue mountains at the edge, the great arch of sky over all. He might have been a young squire at home, overlooking his farms, one eye for the tillage or the upkeep of fence and hedge, another for a covey, or a hare in a farrow. He was as serene as Estéban and as contented; but his comfort lay in easy possession, not in being easily possessed. Occasionally he whistled as he rode, but, like Estéban, broke now and again into a singing voice, more cheerful, I think, than melodious.

"If she be not fair for me,
What care I how fair she be?"

An old song. But Henry Chorley made a tone for it the summer before Mr. Manvers left England, and it had caught his fancy, both the air and the sentiment. They had come aptly to suit his scoffing mood, and to help him salve the wound which a Miss Eleanor Vernon had dealt his heart—a Miss Eleanor Vernon with her clear disdainful eyes. She had given him his first acquaintance with the hot-and-cold disease.

"If she be not fair for me!" Well, she was not to be that. Let her go spin then, and—"What care I how fair she be?" He had discarded her with the Dover cliffs, and resumed possession of himself and his seeing eye. By this time a course of desultory journeying through Brittany and the West of France, a winter in Paris, a packet from Bordeaux to Santander had cured him of his hurt. The song came unsought to his lips, but had no wounded heart to salve.

Mr. Manvers was a pleasant-looking young man, sanguine in hue, grey in the eye, with a twisted sort of smile by no means unattractive. His features were irregular, but he looked wholesome; his humour was fitful, sometimes easy, sometimes unaccountably stiff. They called him a Character at home, meaning that he was liable to freakish asides from the common rotted road, and could not be counted on. It was true. He, for his part, called himself an observer of Manvers, which implied that he had rather watch than take a side; but he was both hot-tempered and quick-tempered, and might well find himself in the middle of things before he knew it. His crooked smile, however, seldom deserted him, seldom was exchanged for a crooked scowl; and the light beard which he had allowed himself in the solitudes of Paris led one to imagine his jaw less square than it really was.

I suppose him to have been five foot ten in his boots, and strong to match. He had a comfortable income, derived from land in Somersetshire, upon which his mother, a widow lady, and his two unmarried sisters lived, and attended archery meetings in company of the curate. The disdain of Miss Eleanor Vernon had cured him of a taste for such simple joys, and now that, by travel, he had cured himself of Miss Eleanor, he was travelling on for his pleasure, or, as he told himself, to avoid the curate. Thus neatly he referred to his obligations to Church and State in Somersetshire.

By six o'clock on this fine May morning he had already ridden far— from Sahagun, indeed, where he had spent some idle days, lounging, and exchanging observations on the weather with the inhabitants. He had been popular, for he was perfectly simple, and without airs; never asked what he did not want to know, and never refused to answer what it was obviously desired he should. But man cannot live upon small talk; and as he had taken up his rest in Sahagun in a moment of impulse—when he saw that it possessed a church-dome covered with glazed green tiles—so now he left it.

"High Heaven!" he had cried, sitting up in bed, "what the deuce am I doing here? Nothing. Nothing on earth. Let's get out of it." So out he had got, and could not ask for breakfast at four in the morning.

He rode fast, desiring to make way before the heat began, and by six o'clock, with the sun above the horizon, was not sorry to see towers and pinnacles, or to hear across the emptiness the clangorous notes of a deep-toned bell. "The muezzin calls the faithful, but for me another summons must be sounded. That town will be Palencia. There I breakfast, by the grace of God. Coffee and eggs."

Palencia it was, a town of pretence, if such a word can be applied to anything Spanish, where things either are or are not, and there's an end. It was as drab as the landscape, as weatherworn and austere; but it had a squat officer sitting at the receipt of custom, which Sahagun had not, and a file of anxious peasants before him, bargaining for their chickens and hay.

Upon the horseman's approach the functionary raised himself, looking over the heads of the crowd as at a greater thing, saluted, and inquired for gate-dues with his patient eyes. "I have here," said Manvers, who loved to be didactic in a foreign language, "a shirt and a comb, the New Testament, the History of the Ingenious Gentleman, Don Quixote de la Mancha, and a toothbrush."

Much of this was Greek to the *doganero*, who, however, understood that the stranger was referring in tolerable Castilian to a provincial gentleman of degree. The name and Manvers' twisted smile together won him the entry. The officer just eased his peaked cap. "Go with God, sir," he directed.

"Assuredly," said Manvers, "but pray assist me to the inn."

The Providencia was named, indicated, and found. There was an elderly man in the yard of it, placidly plucking a live fowl, a barbarity with which our traveller had now ceased to quarrel.

"Leave your horrid task, my friend," he said. "Take my horse, and feed him."

The bird was released, and after shaking, by force of habit, what no longer, or only partially existed, rejoined its companions. They received it coldly, but it soon showed that it could pick as well as be picked.

"Now," said Manvers to the ostler, "give this horse half a feed of corn, then some water, then the other half feed; but give him nothing until you have cooled him down. Do these things, and I present you with one *peseta*. Omit any of them, and I give you nothing at all. Is that a bargain?"

The old man haled off the horse, muttering that it would be a bad bargain for his Grace, to which Manvers replied that we should see. Then he went into the Providencia for his coffee and eggs.

# CHAPTER III

## DIVERSIONS OF TRAVEL

If Sahagun puts you out of conceit with Castile, you are not likely to be put in again by Palencia; for a second-rate town in this kingdom is like a piece of the plain enclosed by a wall, and only emphasises the desolation at the expense of the freedom; and as in a windy square all the city garbage is blown into corners, so the walled town seems to collect and set to festering all the disreputable creatures of the waste.

Mr. Manvers, his meal over, hankered after broad spaces again. He walked the arcaded streets and cursed the flies, he entered the Cathedral and was driven out by the beggars. He leaned over the bridge and watched the green river, and that set him longing for a swim. If his maps told him the truth, some few leagues on the road to Valladolid should discover him a fine wood, the wood of La Huerca, beyond which, skirting it, in fact, should be the Pisuerga. Here he could bathe, loiter away the noon, and take his *merienda*, which should be the best Palencia could supply.

"Muera Marta,
Y muera harta,"

"Let Martha die, but not on an empty stomach," he said to himself. He knew his Don Quixote better than most Spaniards.

He furnished his haversack, then, with bread, ham, sausages, wine and oranges, ordered out his horse, satisfied himself that the ostler had earned his fee, and departed at an ambling pace to seek his amusements. But, though he knew it not, the finger of Fate was upon him, and he was enjoying the last of that perfect leisure without which travel, love-making, the arts and sciences, gardening, or the rearing of a family, are but weariness and disgust. Just outside the gate of Palencia he had an adventure which occupied him until the end of this tale, and, indeed, some way beyond it.

The Puerta de Valladolid is really no gate at all, but a gateway. What walls it may once have pierced have fallen away from it in their fight with time, and now buttresses and rubbish-heaps, a moat of blurred outline and much filth, alone testify to former pretensions. Beyond was to be found a sandy waste, miscalled an *alameda*, a littered place of brown grass, dust and loose stones, fringed with parched acacias, and diversified by hillocks, upon which, in former days of strife, standards may have been placed, mangonels planted, perhaps Napoleonic cannon.

It was upon one of these mounds, which was shaded by a tree, that Manvers observed, and paused in the gateway to observe, the doings of a group of persons, some seven boys and lads, and a girl. A kind of uncouth courtship seemed to be in progress, or (as he put it) the holding of a rude Court. He thought to see a Circe of picaresque Spain with her swinish rout about her. To drop metaphor, the young woman sat upon the hillock, with the half dozen tatterdemalions round her in various stages of amorous enchantment.

He set the girl down for a gipsy, for he knew enough of the country to be sure that no marriageable maiden of worth could be courted in this fashion. Or if not a gipsy then a thing of nought, to be pitied if the truth were known, at any rate to be skirted. Her hair, which seemed to be of a dusty gold tinge, was knotted up in a red handkerchief; her gown was of blue faded to green, her feet were bare. If a gipsy, she was to be trusted to take care of herself; if but a sunburnt vagrant she could be let to shift; and yet he watched her curiously, while she sat as impassive as a young Sphinx, and wondered to himself why he did it.

Suppose her of that sort you may see any day at a fair, jigging outside a booth in red bodice and spangles, a waif, a little who-knows-who, suppose her pretty to death—what is she even then but an iridescent bubble, as one might say, thrown up by some standing pool of vice, as filmy, very nearly as fleeting, and quite as poisonous? It struck him as he watched—not the girl in particular, but a whole genus centred in her—as really extraordinary, as an obliquity of Providence, that such ephemerids must abound, predestined to misery; must come and sin, and wail and go, with souls inside them to be saved, which nobody could save, and bodies fair enough to be loved, which nobody could stoop to love. Had the scheme of our Redemption scope enough for this—for this trifle, along with Santa Teresa, and the Queen of Sheba, and Isabella the Catholic? He perceived himself slipping into the sententious on slight pretence—but presently found himself engaged.

Hatless, shoeless, and coatless were the oafs who surrounded the object of his speculations, some lying flat, with elbows forward and chins to fist; some creeping and scrambling about her to get her notice, or fire her into a rage; some squatting at an easy distance with ribaldries to exchange. But there was one, sitting a little above her on the mound, who seemed to consider himself, in a sort, her proprietor. He was master of the pack, warily on the watch, able by position and strength to prevent what he might at any moment choose to think on infringement of his rights. A sullen, grudging, silent, and jealous dog, Manvers saw him, and asked himself how long she would stand it. At present she seemed unaware of her surroundings.

He saw that she sat broodingly, as if ruminating on more serious things, such as famine or thirst, her elbows on her knees and her face in her two hands. That was the true gipsy attitude, he knew, all the world over. But so intent she was, that she was careless of her person, careless that her bodice was open at the neck and that more people than Manvers were aware of it. A flower was in her mouth, or he thought so, judging from the blot of scarlet thereabouts; her face was set fixedly towards the town—too fixedly that he might care, since she cared so little, whether she saw him there or not. And after all, not she, but the manners of the game centred about her, was what mattered.

Manners, indeed! The fastidious in our young man was all on edge; he became a critic of Spain. Where in England, France, or Italy could you have witnessed such a scene as this? Or what people but the Spaniards among the children of Noah know themselves so certainly lords of the earth that they can treat women, mules, prisoners, Jews, and bulls according to the caprices of appetite? That an Italian should make public display of his property in a woman, or his scorn of her, was a thing unthinkable; yet, if you came to consider it, so it was that a Spaniard should not. Set aside, said he to himself, the grand air, and what has the Spaniard which the brutes have not?

Hotly questioning the attendant heavens, Manvers saw just such an act of mastery, when the lumpish fellow above the girl put his hand upon her, and kept it there, and the others thereupon drew back and ceased their tricks, as if admitting possession had and seisin taken, as the lawyers call it. To Manvers a hateful thing. He felt his blood surge in his neck. "Damn him! I've a mind——! And they pray to a woman!"

But the girl did nothing—neither moved, nor seemed to be aware. Then the drama suddenly quickened, the actors serried, and the acts, down to the climax, followed fast.

Emboldened by her passivity, the oaf advanced by inches, visibly. He looked knowingly about him, collecting approval from his followers, he whispered in her ear, hummed gallant airs, regaled the company with snatches of salt song. Fixed as the Sphinx and unfathomable, she sat on broodingly until, piqued by her indifference, maybe, or swayed by some wave of desire, he caught her round the waist and buried his face in her neck; and then, all at once, she awoke, shivered and collected herself, without warning shook herself free, and hit her bully a blow on the nose with all her force.

He reeled back, with his hands to his face; the blood gushed over his fingers. Then all were on their feet, and a scuffle began, the most unequal you can conceive, and the most impossible. It was all against one, with stones flying and imprecations after them, and in the midst the tawny-haired girl fighting like one possessed.

A minute of this—hardly so much—was more than enough for Manvers, who, when he could believe his eyes, pricked headlong into the fray, and began to lay about him with his crop. "Dogs, sons of dogs, down with your hands!" he cried, in Spanish which was fluent, if imaginative. But his science with the whip was beyond dispute, and the diversion, coming suddenly from behind, scattered the enemy into headlong flight.

The field cleared, the girl was to be seen. She lay moaning on the ground, her arms extended, her right leg twitching. She was bleeding at the ear.

# CHAPTER IV

## TWO ON HORSEBACK

Now, Manvers was under fire; for the enemy, reinforced by stragglers from the town, had unmasked a battery of stones, and was making fine practice from the ruins of the wall. He was hit more than once, his horse more than he; both were exasperated, and he in particular was furious at the presence of spectators who, comfortably in the shade, watched, and had been watching, the whole affair with enviable detachment of mind and body. With so much to chafe him, he may be pardoned for some irritability.

He dismounted as coolly as he could, and led his horse about to cover her from the stones. "Come," he said, as he stooped to touch her, "I must move you out of this. Saint Stephen—blessed young man—has forestalled this particular means of going to Heaven. Oh, damn the stones!"

He used no ceremony, but picked her up as if she had been a dressmaker's dummy, and set her on her feet, where, after swaying about, and some balancing with her hands, she presently steadied herself, and stood, dazed and empty-eyed. Her cheek was cut, her ear was bleeding; her hair was down, the red handkerchief uncoiled; her dusky skin was stained with dirt and scratches, and her bosom heaved riotously as she caught for her breath.

"Take your time, my dear," said Manvers kindly. And she did, by tumbling into his arms. Here, then, was a situation for the student of Manners; a brisk discharge of stones from an advancing line of skirmishers, a strictly impartial crowd of sightseers, a fidgety horse, and himself embarrassed by a girl in a faint.

He called for help and, getting none, shook his fist at the callous devils who ignored him; he inspected his charge, who looked as pure as a child in her swoon, all her troubles forgotten and sins blotted out; he inquired of the skies, as if hopeful that the ravens, as of old, might bring him help; at last, seeing nothing else for it, he picked up the girl in both arms and pitched her on to the saddle. There, with some adjusting, he managed to prop her while he led the horse slowly away. He had to get the reins in his teeth before he had gone ten yards. The retreat began.

It was within two hours of noon, or nothing had saved him from a retirement as harassing as Sir John Moore's. It was the sun, not ravens, that came to his help. Meantime the girl had recovered herself somewhat, and, when they were out of sight of the town and its inhabitants, showed him that she had by sliding from the saddle and standing firmly on her feet.

"Hulloa!" said Manvers. "What's the matter now? Do you think you can walk back? You can't, you know." He addressed her in his best Castilian. "I am afraid you are hurt. Let me help——" but she held him off with a stiffening arm, while she wiped her face with her petticoat, and put herself into some sort of order.

She did it deftly and methodically, with the practised hands of a woman used to the public eye. She might have been an actress at the wings, about to go on. Nor would she look at him or let him see that she was aware of his presence until all was in order—her hair twisted into the red handkerchief, the neck of her dress pinned together, her torn skirt nicely hung. Her coquetry, her skill in adjusting what seemed past praying for, her pains with herself, were charming to see and very touching. Manvers watched her closely and could not deny her beauty.

She was a vivid beauty, fiercely coloured, with her tawny gold hair, sunburnt skin, and jade-green, far-seeing eyes, her coiled crimson handkerchief and blue-green gown. She was finely made, slim, and in contour hardly more than a child; and yet she seemed to him very mature, a practised hand, with very various knowledge deep in her eyes, and a wide acquaintance behind her quiet lips. With her re-ordered toilette she had taken on self-possession and dignity, a reserve which baffled him. Without any more reason than this he felt for her a kind of respect which nothing, certainly, in what he had seen of her circumstances could justify. Yet he gave her her title—which marks his feeling.

"Señorita," he said, "I wish to be of service to you. Command me. Shall I take you back to Palencia?"

She answered him seriously. "I beg that you will not, sir."

"If you have friends——" he began, and she said at once, "I have none."

"Or parents——"

"None."

"Relatives——"

"None, none."

"Then your——"

"I know what you would say. I have no house."

"Then," said Manvers, looking vaguely over the plain, "what do you wish me to do for you?"

She was now sitting by the roadside, very collectedly looking down at her hands in her lap. "You will leave me here, if you must," she said; "but I would ask your charity to take me a little farther from Palencia. Nobody has ever been kind to me before."

She said this quite simply, as if stating a fact. He was moved.

"You were unhappy in Palencia?"

"Yes," she said, "I would rather be left here." The enormous plain of Castile, treeless, sun-struck, empty of living thing, made her words eloquent.

"Absurd," said Manvers. "If I leave you here you will die."

"In Palencia," said the girl, "I cannot die." And then her grave eyes pierced him, and he knew what she meant.

"Great God!" said Manvers. "Then I shall take you to a convent."

She nodded her head. "Where you will, sir," she replied. Her gravity, far beyond her seeming station, gave value to her confidence.

"That seems to me the best thing I can do with you," Manvers said; "and if you don't shirk it, there is no reason why I should. Now, can you stick on the saddle if I put you up?"

She nodded again. "Up you go then." He would have swung her up sideways, lady-fashion; but she laughed and cried, "No, no," put a hand on his shoulder, her left foot in the stirrup, and swung herself into the saddle as neatly as a groom. There she sat astride, like a circus-rider, and stuck her arm akimbo as she looked down for his approval.

"Bravo," said Manvers. "You have been a-horseback before this, my girl. Now you must make room for me." He got up behind her and took the reins from under her arm. With the other arm it was necessary to embrace her; she allowed it sedately. Then they ambled off together, making a Darby and Joan affair of it.

But the sun was now close upon noon, burning upon them out of a sky of brass. There was no wind, and the flies were maddening. After a while he noticed that the girl simply stooped her head to the heat, as if she were wilting like a picked flower. When he felt her heavy on his arm he saw that he must stop. So he did, and plied her with wine from his pocket-flask, feeding her drop by drop as she lay back against him. He got bread out of his haversack and made her eat; she soon revived, and then he learned the fact that she had eaten nothing since yesterday's noon. "How should I eat," she asked, "when I have earned nothing?"

"Nohow, but by charity," he agreed. "Had Palencia no compassion?" She grew dark and would not answer him at first; presently asked, had he not seen Palencia?

"I agree," he said. "But let me ask you, if I may without indiscretion, how did you propose to earn your bread in Palencia?"

"I would have worked in the fields for a day, sir," she told him; "but not longer, for I have to get on."

"Where do you wish to go?"

"Away from here."

"To Valladolid?"

She looked up into his face—her head was still near his shoulder. "To Valladolid? Never there."

This made him laugh. "To Palencia? Never there. To Valladolid? Never there. Where then, lady of the sea-green eyes?"

She veiled her eyes quickly. "To Madrid, I suppose. I wish to work."

"Can you find work there?"

"Surely. It is a great city."

"Do you know it?"

"Yes, I was there long ago."

"What did you do there?"

"I worked. I was very well there." She sat up and looked back over his shoulder. She had done that once or twice before, and now he asked her what she was looking for. She desisted at once: "Nothing" was her answer.

He made her drink from the flask again and gave her his pocket handkerchief to cover her head. When she understood she laughed at him without disguise. Did he think she feared the sun? She bade him look at her neck—which was walnut brown, and sleek as satin; but when he would have taken back his handkerchief she refused to give it, and put it over her head like a hood, and tied it under her chin. She then turned herself round to face him. "Is it so you would have it, sir?" she asked, and looked bewitching.

"My dear," said Manvers, "you are a beauty." Shall he be blamed if he kissed her? Not by me, since she never blamed him.

Her clear-seeing eyes searched his face; her kissed mouth looked very serious, and also very pure. Then, as he observed her ardently, she coloured and looked down, and afterwards turned herself the way they were to go, and with a little sigh settled into his arm.

Manvers spurred his horse, and for some time nothing was said between them. But he was of a talkative habit, with a trick of conversing with himself for lack of a better man. He asked her if he was forgiven, and felt her answer on his arm, though she gave him none in words. This was not to content him. "I see that you will not," he said, to tease her. "Well, I call that hard after my stoning. I had believed the ladies of Spain kinder to their cavaliers than to grudge a kiss for a cartload of stones at the head. Well, well, I'm properly paid. Laws go as kings will, I know. God help poor men!" He would have gone on with his baiting had she not surprised him.

She turned him a burning face. "Caballero, caballero, have done!" she begged him. "You rescued me from worse than death—and what could I deny you? See, sir, I have lived fifteen, seventeen years in the world, and nobody—nobody, I say—has ever done me a kindness before. And you think that I grudge you!" She was really unhappy, and had to be comforted.

They became close friends after that. She told him her name was Manuela, and that she was Valencian by birth. A Gitana? No, indeed. She was a Christian. "You are a very bewitching Christian, Manuela," he told her, and drew her face back, and kissed her again. I am told that there's nothing in kissing, once: it's the second time that counts. In the very act— for eyes met as well as lips—he noticed that hers wavered on the way to his, beyond him, over the road they had travelled; and the ceremony over, he again asked her why. She passed it off as before, saying that she had looked at nothing, and begged him to go forward.

Ahead of them now, through the crystalline flicker of the heat, he saw the dark rim of the wood, the cork forest of La Huerca for which he was looking, and which hid the river from his aching eyes. No foot-burnt wanderer in Sahara ever hailed his oasis with heartier thanksgiving; but it was still a league and a half away. He addressed himself to the task of reaching it, and we may suppose Manuela respected his efforts. At any rate, there was silence between the pair for the better part of an hour—what time the unwinking sun, vertically overhead, deprived them of so much as the sight of their own shadows, and drove the very crows with wings adust to skulk in the furrows. The shrilling of crickets, the stumbling hoofs of an overtaxed horse, and the creaking of saddle and girth made a din in the deadly stillness of this fervent noon, and, since there was no other sound to be heard, it is hard to tell how Manvers was aware of a traveller behind him, unless he was served by the sixth sense we all have, to warn as that we are not alone.

Sure enough, when he looked over his shoulder, he was aware of a donkey and his rider drawing smoothly and silently near. The pair of them were so nearly of the colour of the ground, he had to look long to be sure; and as he looked, Manuela suddenly leaned sideways and saw what he saw. It was just as if she had received a stroke of the sun. She stiffened; he felt the thrill go through her; and when she resumed her first position she was another person.

# CHAPTER V

## THE AMBIGUOUS THIRD

"God save your grace," said Estéban; for it was he who, sitting well back upon his donkey's rump, with exceedingly bright eyes and a cheerful grin, now forged level with Manvers and his burdened steed.

Manvers gave him a curt "Good-day," and thought him an impudent fellow—which was not justified by anything Estéban had done. He had been discretion itself; and, indeed, to his eyes there had been nothing of necessity remarkable in the pair on the horse. If a lady—Duchess or baggage—happened to be sharing the gentleman's saddle, an arrangement must be presumed, which could not possibly concern himself. That is the reasonable standpoint of a people who mind their own business and credit their neighbours with the same preoccupation.

But Manvers was an Englishman, and could not for the life of him consider Estéban as anything but a puppy for seeing him in a compromising situation. So much was he annoyed that he did not remark any longer that Manuela was another person, sitting stiffly, strained against his arm, every muscle on the stretch, as taut as a ship's cable in the tideway, her face in rigid profile to the newcomer.

Estéban was in no way put out. "Many good days light upon your grace!" he cheerfully repeated—so cheerfully that Manvers was appeased.

"Good-day, good-day to you," he said. "You ride light and I ride heavy, otherwise you had not overtaken us."

Estéban showed his fine teeth, and waved his hand towards the hazy distance; from the tail of his eye he watched Manuela in profile. "Who knows that, sir? *Lo que ha de ser*—as we say. Ah, who knows that?" Manuela strained her face forward.

"Well," said Manvers, "I do, for example. I have proved my horse. He's a Galician, and a good goer. It would want a brave *borico* to outpace him."

Estéban slipped into the axiomatic, as all Spaniards will. "There's a providence of the road, sir, and a saint in charge of travellers. And we know, sir, *a cada puerco viene su San Martin.*" Manuela stooped her body forward, and peered ahead, as one strains to see in the dark.

"Your proverb is oddly chosen, it seems to me," said Manvers.

Estéban gave a little chuckle from his throat.

"A proverb is a stone flung into a pack of starlings. It may scare the most, but may hit one. By mine I referred to the ways of providence, under a figure. Destiny is always at work."

"No doubt," said Manvers, slightly bored.

"It might have been your destiny to have outpaced me: the odds were with you. On the other hand, as you have not, it must have been mine to have overtaken you."

"You are a philosopher?" asked Manvers, fatigue deliberately in his voice. Estéban's eyes shone intensely; he had marked the changed inflection.

"I studied the Humanities at Salamanca," he said carelessly. "That was when I was an innocent. Since then I have learned in a harder school. I am learning still—every day I learn something new. I am a gentleman born, as your grace has perceived: why not a philosopher?"

Manvers was rather ashamed of himself. "Of course, of course! Why not indeed? I am very glad to see you, while our ways coincide."

Estéban raised his battered straw. "I kiss the feet of your grace, and hope your grace's lady"—Manuela quivered—"is not disturbed by my company; for to tell you the truth, sir, I propose to enjoy your own as long as you and she are agreeable. I am used to companionship." He shot a keen glance at Manuela, who never moved.

"She will speak for herself, no doubt," said Manvers; but she did not. The gleam in Estéban's light eyes gave point to his next speech.

"I have a notion that the señora is not of your mind, sir," he said, "and am sorry. I can hardly remain as an unwelcome third in a journey. It would be a satisfaction to me if the señora would assure me that I am wrong." Manuela now turned her head with an effort and looked down upon the grinning youth.

"Why should I care whether you stay or go?" she said. Her eyelids flickered over her eyes as though he were dust in their light. He showed his teeth.

"Why indeed, señora? God knows I have no reputation to bring you, though the company of a gentleman, the son of a gentleman, never comes amiss, they say. But two is company, and three is a fair. I have found it so, and so doubtless has your ladyship."

She made him no answer, and had turned away her face long before he had finished. After that the conversation was mainly of his making; for Manuela would say nothing, and Manvers had nothing to say. The cork wood was plain in front of him now; he thanked God for the prospect of food and rest. In fifteen minutes, thought he, he should be swimming in the Pisuerga.

The forest began tentatively, with heath, sparse trees and mounds of cistus and bramble. Manvers followed the road, which ran through a portion of it, until he saw the welcome thickets on either hand, deep tunnels of dark and shadowy places where the sun could not stab; then he turned aside over the broken ground, and Estéban's donkey picked a dainty way behind him. When he had reached what seemed to him perfection, he pulled up.

"Now, young lady," he said; "I will give you food and drink, and then you shall go to sleep, and so will I. Afterwards we will consider what had best be done with you."

"Yes, sir," she replied in a whisper. Manvers dismounted and held out his hand to her. There was no more coquetting with the saddle. She scarcely touched his hand, and did not once lift her eyes to him—but he was busy with his haversack and had no thoughts for her.

Estéban meantime sat the donkey, looking gravely at his company, blinking his eyes, smiling quietly, recurring now and then to the winding minor air which had been in his head all day. He was perfectly unhampered by any doubts of his welcome, and watched with serious attention the preparations for a meal in the open which Manvers was making with the ease and despatch of one versed in camps.

Ham and sausage, rolls of bread, a lettuce, oranges, cheese, dates, a bottle of wine, another of water, salt, olives, a knife and fork, a plate, a corkscrew; every article was in its own paper, some were marked in pencil what they were. All were spread out upon a horse-blanket; in good enough order for a field-inspection. Nothing was wanting, and Estéban was as keen as a wolf. Even Manvers rubbed his hands. He looked shrewdly at his neighbour.

"Good *alforjas*, eh?"

"Excellent indeed, sir," said Estéban hoarsely. It was hard to see this food, and know that he could not eat of it. Manuela was sitting under a tree, her face in her hands.

"How far away," said Manvers, "is the water, do you suppose?"

The water? Estéban collected himself with a start. The water? He jerked his head towards the display on the blanket. "It is under your hand, caballero. That bottle, I take it, holds water."

Manvers laughed. "Yes, yes. I mean the river. I am going to swim in the river. Don't wait for me." He turned to the girl. "Take some food, my friend. I'll be back before long."

Her swift transitions bewildered him. She showed him now a face of extreme terror. She was on her feet in a moment, rigid, and her eyes were so pale that her face looked empty of eyes, like a mask. What on earth was the matter with her? He understood her to be saying, "I must go where you go. I must never leave you———" words like that; but they came from her mouthed rather than voiced, as the babbling of a mad woman. All that was clear was that she was beside herself with fright. Looking to Estéban for an explanation, he surprised a triumphant gleam in that youth's light eyes, and saw him grinning—as a dog grins, with the lip curled back.

But Estéban spoke. "I think the lady is right, sir. Affection is a beautiful thing." He added politely, "The loss will be mine."

Manvers looked from one to the other of these curious persons, so clearly conscious of each other, yet so strict to avoid recognition. His eyes rested on Manuela. "What's the matter, my child?" She met his glance furtively, as if afraid that he was angry; plainly she was ashamed of her panic. Her eyes were now collected, her brow cleared, and the tension of her arms relaxed.

"Nothing is the matter," she said in a low voice. "I will stay here." She was shaking still; she held herself with both her hands, and shook the more.

"I think that you are knocked over by the heat and all the rest of your troubles," said Manvers, "and I don't wonder. Repose yourself here—eat—drink. Don't spare the victuals, I beg. And as for you, my brother, I invite you too to eat what you please. And I place this young lady in your charge. Don't forget that. She's had a fright, and good reason for it; she's been hurt. I leave her in your care with every confidence that you will protect her."

Every word spoken was absorbed by Estéban with immense relish. The words pleased him, to begin with, by their Spanish ring. Manvers had been pleased himself. It was the longest speech he had yet made in Castilian; but he had no notion, of course, how exquisitely apposite to the situation they were.

Estéban became superb. He rose to the height of the argument, and to that of his inches, took off his old hat and held it out the length of his arm. "Let the lady fear nothing, señor caballero of my soul. I engage the honour of a gentleman that she shall have every consideration at my hands which her virtues merit. No more"—he looked at the sullen beauty between him and the Englishman—"No more, for that would be idolatrous; and no less, for that would be injustice. *Vaya, señor caballero, vaya V^d con Dios.*" Manvers nodded and strolled away.

# CHAPTER VI

## A SPANISH CHAPTER

His removal snapped a chain. These two persons became themselves.

Manuela with eyes ablaze strode over to Estéban. "Well," she said. "You have found me. What is your pleasure?"

He sat very still on his donkey, watching her. He rolled himself a cigarette, still watching, and as he lighted it, looked at her over the flame.

"Speak, Estéban," she said, quivering; but he took two luxurious inhalations first, discharged in dense columns through his nose. Then he said, breathing smoke, "I have come to kill you, Manuelita—from Pobledo in a day and a half."

She had folded her arms, and now nodded. "I know it. I have expected you."

"Of course," said Estéban, inhaling enormously. He shot the smoke upwards towards the light, where it floated and spread out in radiant bars of blue. Manuela was tapping her foot.

"Well, I am here," she said. "I might have left you, but I have not. Why don't you do what you intend?"

"There is plenty of time," said Estéban, and continued to smoke. He began to make another cigarette.

"Do you know why I chose to stay with you?" she asked him softly. "Do you know, Estéban?"

He raised his eyebrows. "Not at all."

"It was because I had a bargain to make with you."

He looked at her inquiringly; but he shrugged. "It will be a hard bargain for you, my girl," he told her.

"I believe you will agree to it," she said quickly, "seeing that of my own will I have remained here. I will let you kill me as you please—on a condition."

"Name your condition," said Estéban. "I will only say now that it is my wish to strangle you with my hands."

She put both hers to her throat. "Good," she said. "That shall be your affair. But let the caballero go free. He has done you no harm."

"On the contrary," said Estéban, "I shall certainly kill him when he returns. Have no doubt of that. Then I shall have his horse."

Immediately, without fear, she went up to him where he sat his donkey. She saw the knife in his *faja*, but had no fear at all. She came quite close to him, with an ardent face, with eyes alight. She stretched out her arms like a man on a cross.

"Kill, kill, Estéban! But listen first. You shall spare that gentleman's life, for he has done you no wrong."

He laughed her down. "Wrong! And you come to me to swear that on the Cross of Christ? Daughter of swine, you lie."

Tears were in her eyes, which made her blink and shake her head— but she came closer yet in a passion of entreaty. She was so close that her bosom touched him. "Kill, Estéban, kill—but love me first!" Her arms were about him now, as if she must have love of him or die. "Estéban, Estéban!" she was whispering as if she hungered and thirsted for him. He shivered at a memory. "Love me once, love me once, Estéban!" Closer and closer she clung to him; her eyes implored a kiss.

"Loose me, you jade," he said, less sharply, but she clove the closer to him, and one hand crept downwards from his shoulder, as if she would embrace him by the middle. "Too late, Manuelita, too late," he said again, but he was plainly softening. She drew his face towards hers as if to kiss him, then whipped the long knife out of his girdle and drove it with all her sobbing force into his neck. Estéban uttered a thick groan, threw his head up and rocked twice. Then his head dropped, and he fell sideways off his donkey.

She stood staring at what she had done.

# CHAPTER VII

## THE SLEEPER AWAKENED

Manvers returned whistling from his bath, at peace with all the world of Spain, in a large mood of benevolence and charitable judgment. His mind dwelt pleasantly on Manuela, but pity mixed with his thought; and he added some prudence on his own account. "That child—she's no more—I must do something for her. Not a bad 'un, I'll swear, not fundamentally bad. I don't doubt her as I doubt the male: he's too glib by half... She's distractingly pretty—what nectarine colour! The mouth of a child—that droop at the corners—and as soft as a child's too." He shook his head. "No more kissing or I shall be in a mess."

When he reached his tree and his luncheon, to find his companions gone, he was a little taken aback. His genial proposals were suddenly chilled. "Queer couple—I had a notion that they knew something of each other. So they've made a match of it."

Then he saw a brass crucifix lying in the middle of his plate. "Hulloa!" He stooped to pick it up. It was still warm. He smiled and felt a glow come back. "Now that's charming of her. That's a pretty touch—from a pretty girl. She's no baggage, depend upon it." The string had plainly hung the thing round her neck, the warmth was that of her bosom. He held it tenderly while he turned it about. "I'll warrant now, that was all she had upon her. Not a maravedi beside. I know it's the last thing to leave 'em. I'm repaid, more than repaid. I'll wear you for a bit, my friend, if you won't scorch a heretic." Here he slipped the string over his head, and dropped the cross within his collar. "I'll treat you to a chain in Valladolid," was his final thought before he consigned Manuela to his cabinet of memories.

He poured and drank, hacked at his ham-bone and ate. "By the Lord," he went on commenting, "they've not had bite or sup. Too busy with their match-making? Too delicate to feast without invitation? Which?" He pondered the puzzle. He had invited Manuela, he was sure: had he included her swain? If not, the thing was clear. She wouldn't eat without him, and he couldn't eat without his host. It was the best thing he knew of Estéban.

He finished his meal, filled and lit a pipe, smoked half of it drowsily, then lay and slept. Nothing disturbed his three hours' rest, not even the gathering cloud of flies, whose droning over a neighbouring thicket must have kept awake a lighter sleeper. But Manvers was so fast that he did not hear footsteps in the wood, nor the sound of picking in the peaty ground.

It was four o'clock and more when he awoke, sat up and looked at his watch. Yawning and stretching at ease, he then became aware of a friar, with a brown shaven head and fine black beard, who was digging near by. This man, whose eyes had been upon him, waiting for recognition, immediately stopped his toil, struck his spade into the ground, and came towards him, bowing as he came.

"Good evening, señor caballero," he said. "I am Fray Juan de la Cruz, at your service; from the convent of N. S. de la Peña near by. I have to be my own grave-digger; but will you be so obliging as to commit the body while I read the office?"

To this abrupt invitation Manvers could only reply by staring. Fray Juan apologised.

"I imagined that you had perceived my business," he said, "which truly is none of yours. It will be an act of charity on your part—therefore its own reward."

"May I ask you," said Manvers, now on his feet, "what, or whom, you are burying?"

"Come," the friar replied. "I will show you the body." Manvers followed him into the thicket.

"Good God, what's this?" The staring light eyes of Estéban Vincaz had no reply for him. He had to turn away, sick at the sight.

Fray Juan de la Cruz told him what he knew. A young girl, riding an ass, had come to the church of the convent, where he happened to be, cleaning the sanctuary. The Reverend Prior was absent, the brothers were afield. She was in haste, she said, and the matter would not allow of delay. She reported that she had killed a man in the wood of La Huerca, to save the life of a gentleman who had been kind to her, who had, indeed, but recently imperilled his own for hers. "If you doubt me," she had said, "go to the forest, to such and such a part. There you will find the gentleman asleep. He has a crucifix of mine. The dead man lies not far away, with his own knife near him, with which I killed him. Now," she had said, "I trust you to report all I have said to that gentleman, for I must be off."

"Good God!" said Manvers again.

"God indeed is the only good," said Fray Juan, "and His ways past finding out. But I have no reason to doubt this girl's story. She told me, moreover, the name of the man—or his names, as you may say."

"Had he more than one then?" Manvers asked him, but without interest. The dead was nothing to him, but the deed was much. This wild girl, who had been sleek and kissing but a few hours before, now stood robed in tragic weeds, fell purpose in her green eyes! And her child's mouth—stretched to murder! And her youth—hardy enough to stab!

"The unfortunate young man," said Fray Juan, "was the son of a more unfortunate father; but the name that he used was not that of his house. His father, it seems——" but Manvers stopped him.

"Excuse me—I don't care about his father or his names. Tell me anything more that the girl had to say."

"I have told you everything, señor caballero," said Fray Juan; "and I will only add that you are not to suppose that I am violating the confidences of God. Far from that. She made no confession in the true sense, though she promised me that she would not fail to do so at the earliest moment. I had it urgently from herself that I should seek you out with her tale, and rehearse it to you. In justice to her, I am now to ask you if it is true, so far as you are concerned in it?"

Manvers replied, "It's perfectly true. I found her in bad company at Palencia; a pack of ruffians was about her, and she might have been killed. I got her out of their hands, knocked about and wounded, and brought her so far on the road to the first convent I could come at. That poor devil there overtook us about a league from the wood. She had nothing to say to him, nor he to her, but I remember noticing that she didn't seem happy after he had joined us. He had been her lover, I suppose?"

"She gave me to understand that," said Fray Juan gravely. Manvers here started at a memory.

"By the Lord," he cried, "I'll tell you something. When we got to the wood I wanted to bathe in the river, and was going to leave those two together. Well, she was in a taking about that. She wanted to come with me—there was something of a scene." He recalled her terror, and Estéban's snarling lip. "I might have saved all this—but how was I to know? I blame myself. But what puzzles me still is why the man should have wanted my life. Can you explain that?"

Fray Juan was discreet. "Robbery," he suggested, but Manvers laughed.

"I travel light," he said. "He must have seen that I was not his game. No, no," he shook his head. "It couldn't have been robbery."

Fray Juan, I say, was discreet; and it was no business of his.... But it was certainly in his mind to say that Estéban need not have been the robber, nor Manvers' portmanteau the booty. However, he was silent, until the Englishman muttered, "God in Heaven, what a country!" and then he took up his parable.

"All countries are very much the same, as I take it, since God made them all together, and put man up to be the master of them, and took the woman out of his side to be his blessing and curse at once. The place whence she was taken, they say, can never fully be healed until she is restored to it; and when that is done, it is not a certain cure. Such being the plan of this world, it does not become us to quarrel with its manifestations here or there. Señor caballero, if you are ready I will proceed. Assistance at the feet, a handful of earth at the proper moment are all I shall ask of you." He slipped a surplice over his head. The office was said.

"Fray Juan," said Manvers at the end, "will you take this trifle from me? A mass, I suppose, for that poor devil's soul would not come amiss."

Fray Juan took that as a sign of grace, and was glad that he had held his tongue. "Far from it," he said, "it would be extremely proper. It shall be offered, I promise you."

"Now," said Manvers after a pause, "I wonder if you can tell me this. Which way did she go off?"

Fray Juan shook his head. "No lo sé. She came to me in the church, and spoke, and passed like the angel of death. May she go with God!"

"I hope so," said Manvers. Then he looked into the placid face of the brown friar. "But I must find her somehow." Upon that addition he shut his mouth with a snap. The survey which he had to endure from Fray Juan's patient eyes was the best answer to it.

"Oh, but I must, you know," he said.

"Better not, my son," said Fray Juan. "It seems to me that you have seen enough. Your motives will be misunderstood."

Manvers laughed. "They are rather obscure to me—but I can't let her pay for my fault."

"You may make her pay double," said Fray Juan.

"No," said Manvers decisively, "I won't. It's my turn to pay now."

The Friar shrugged. "It is usually the woman who pays. But *lo que ha de ser...!*"

The everlasting phrase! "That proverb serves you well in Spain, Fray Juan," said Manvers, who was in a staring fit.

"It is all we have that matters. Other nations have to learn it; here we know it."

Manvers mounted his horse and stooping from the saddle, offered his hand. "Adios, Fray Juan."

"Vaya V<sup>d</sup> con Dios!" said the friar, and watched him away. "Pobrecita!" he said to himself—"unhappy Manuela!"

# CHAPTER VIII

## REFLECTIONS OF AN ENGLISHMAN

But Manvers was well upon his way, riding with squared jaw, with rein and spur towards Valladolid. He neither whistled nor chanted to the air; he was *vacuus viator* no longer, travelled not for pleasure but to get over the leagues. For him this country of distances and great air was not Castile, but Broceliande; a land of enchantments and pain. He was no longer fancy-free, but bound to a quest.

Consider the issues of this day of his. From bathing in pastoral he had been suddenly soused into tragedy's seething-pot. His idyll of the tanned gipsy, with her glancing eyes and warm lips, had been spattered out with a brushful of blood; the scene was changed from sunny life to wan death. Here were the staring eyes of a dead man, and his mouth twisted awry in its last agony. He could not away with the shock, nor divest himself of a share in it. If he, by mischance, had taken up with Manuela, he had taken up with Estéban too.

The vanished players in the drama loomed in his mind larger for that fateful last act. The tragic sock and the mask enhanced them. What mystery lay behind Manuela's sidelong eyes? What sin or suffering? What knowledge, how gained, justified Estéban's wizened saws? These two were wise before their time; when they ought to have been flirting on the brink of life, here they were, breasting the great flood, familiar with death, hating and stabbing!

A pretty child with a knife in her hand; and a boy murdered—what a country! And where stood he, Manvers, the squire of Somerset, with his thirty years, his University education and his seat on the bench? Exactly level with the curate, to be counted on for an archery meeting! Well enough for diversion; but when serious affairs were on hand, sent out of the way. Was it not so, that he, as the child of the party, was dismissed to bathe while his elders fought out their deadly quarrel? I put it in the interrogative; but he himself smarted under the answer to it, and although he never formulated the thought, and made no plans, and could make none, I have no doubt but that his wounded self-esteem, seeking a salve, found it in the assurance that he would protect Manuela from the consequences of her desperate act; that his protection was his duty and her need. The English mind works that way; we cannot endure a breath upon our fair surface. We must direct the operations of this world, or the devil's in it.

Manvers was not, of course, in love with Manuela. He was sentimentally engaged in her affairs, and very sure that they were, and must be, his own. Yet I don't know whether the waking dream which he had upon the summit of that plateau of brown rock which bounds Valladolid upon the north was the cause or consequence of his implication.

He had climbed this sharp ridge because a track wavered up it which cut off some miles of the road. It was not easy going by any means, but the view rewarded him. The land stretched away to the four quarters of the compass and disappeared into a copper-brown haze. He stood well above the plain, which seemed infinite. Corn-land and waste, river-bed and moor, were laid out below him as in a geographer's model. He thought that he stood up there apart, contemplating time and existence. He was indeed upon the convex of the world, projecting from it into illimitable space, consciously sharing its mighty surge.

This did not belittle him. On the contrary, he felt something of the helmsman's pride, something of the captain's on the bridge. He was driving the world. He soared, perched up there, apart from men and their concerns. All Spain lay at his feet; he marked the way it must go. It was possible for him now to watch a man crawl, like a maggot, from his cradle, and urge a painful way to his grave. And, to his exalted eye, from cradle to grave was but a span's length.

From such sublime investigation it was but a step to sublimity itself. His soul seemed separate from his body; he was dispassionate, superhuman, all-seeing and all-comprehending. Now he could see men as winged ants, crossing each other, nearing, drifting apart, interweaving, floating in a cloud, blown high, blown low by wafts of air; and here, presently, came one Manvers, and there, driven by a gust, went another, Manuela.

At these two insects, as one follows idly one gull out of a flock, he could look with interest, and without emotion. He saw them drift, touch and part, and each be blown its way, helpless mote in the dust of the great plain. From one to the other he turned his eyes. The Manvers gnat flew the straighter course, holding to an upper current; the Manuela wavered, but tended ever to a lower plane. The wind from the mountains of Asturias freshened and blew over him. In a singular moment of divination he saw the two insects of his vision caught in the draught and whirled together again. A spiral flight upwards was begun; in ever-narrowing circles they climbed, bid fair to soar. They reached a steadier stream, they sped along together; but then, as a gust took them, they dipped below it and steadily declined, wavering, whirling about each other. Down and down they went, until they were lost to his eye in the dust of heat. He saw them no more.

Manvers came to himself, and shook his senses back into his head. The sun was sinking over Portugal, the evening wind was chill. Had he been dreaming? What sense of fate was upon him? "Come up, Rosinante, take me out of the cave of Montesinos." He guided his horse in and out of the boulder-strewn track to the edge of the plateau; and there before him, many leagues away, like a patch of whitewash splodged down upon a blue field, lay Valladolid, the city of burning and pride.

UPON A BLUE FIELD LAY VALLADOLID.

**The towers of Segovia.**

# CHAPTER IX

## A VISIT TO THE JEWELLER'S

If God in His majesty made the Spains and the nations which people them, perhaps it was His mercy that convoked the Spanish cities—as His servant Philip piled rock upon rock and called it Madrid—and made cesspits for the cleansing of the country.

Behold the Castilian, the Valencian, the Murcian on his glebe, you find an exact relation established; the one exhales the other. The man is what his country is, tragic, hag-ridden, yet impassive, patient under the sun. He stands for the natural verities. You cannot change him, move, nor hurt him. He can earn neither your praises nor reproach. As well might you blame the staring noon of summer or throw a kind word to the everlasting hills. The bleak pride of the Castillano, the flint and steel of Aragon, the languor which veils Andalusian fire—travelling the lands which gave them birth, you find them scored in large over mountain and plain and riverbed, and bitten deep into the hearts of the indwellers. They are as seasonable there as the flowers of waste places, and will charm you as much. So Spanish travel is one of the restful relaxations, because nothing jars upon you. You feel that you are assisting a destiny, not breaking it. Not discovery is before you so much as realisation.

But in the city Spanish blood festers, and all that seemed plausible in the open air is now monstrous, full of vice and despair. Whereas, outside, the man stood like a rock, and let Fate seam or bleach him bare; here, within walls, he rages, shows his teeth, blasphemes, or sinks into sloth. You will find him heaped against the walls like ordure, hear him howl for blood in the bull-ring, appraise women, as if they were dainties, in the *alamedas*, loaf, scratch, pry where none should pry, go begging with his sores, trade his own soul for his mother's. His pride becomes insolence, his tragedy hideous revolt, his impassivity swinish, his rock of sufficiency a rook of offence. God in His mercy, or the Devil in his despite, made the cities of Spain.

And yet the man, so superbly at his ease in his enormous spaces, is his own conclusion when he goes to town; the permutation is logical. He is too strong a thing to break his nature; it will be aggravated but not deflected. Leave him to swarm in the *plaza* and seek his nobler brother. Go out by the gate, descend the winding suburb, which gives you the burnt plains and far blue hills, now on one hand, now on the other, as you circle down and down, with the walls mounting as you fall; touch once more the dusty earth, traverse the deep shade of the ilex-avenue; greet the ox-teams, the filing mules, as they creep up the hill to the town: you are bound for their true, great Spain. And though it may be ten days since you saw it, or fifty years, you will find nothing altered. The Spaniard is still the flower of his rocks. *O dura tellus Iberiae!*

From the window of his garret Don Luis Ramonez de Alavia could overlook the town wall, and by craning his neck out sideways could have seen, if he had a mind, the cornice-angle of the palace of his race. It was a barrack in these days, and had been so since ruin had settled down on the Ramonez with the rest of Valladolid. That had been in the sixteenth century, but no Ramonez had made any effort to repair it. Every one of them did as Don Luis was doing now, and accepted misery in true Spanish fashion. Not only did he never speak of it, he never thought of it either. It was; therefore it had to be.

He rose at dawn, every day of his life, and took his sop in coffee in his bedgown, sitting on the edge of his bed. He heard mass in the Church of Las Angustias, in the same chapel at the same hour. Once a month he communicated, and then the sop was omitted. He was shaved in the barber's shop—Gomez the Sevillian kept it—at the corner of the *plaza*. Gomez, the little dapper, black-eyed man, was a friend of his, his newspaper and his doctor.

He took a high line with Gomez, as you may when you owe a man twopence a week.

That over, he took the sun in the *plaza*, up and down the centre line of flags in fine weather, up and down the arcade if it rained. He saw the *diligence* from Madrid come in, he saw the *diligence* for Madrid go out. He knew, and accepted the salutes of every *arriero* who worked in and out of the city, and passed the time of day with Micael the lame water-seller, who never failed to salute him.

At noon he ate an onion and a piece of cheese, and then he dozed till three. As the clock of the University struck that hour he put on his *capa*—summer and winter he wore it, with melancholy and good reason; by ten minutes past he was entering the shop of Sebastian the goldsmith, in the Plaza San Benito, in the which he sat till dusk, motionless and absorbed in thought, talking little, seeming to observe little, and yet judging everything in the light of strong common sense.

Summer or winter, at dusk he arose, flecked a mote or two of dust from his *capa*, seated his beaver upon his grey head, grasped his malacca, and departed with a "Be with God, my friend." To this Sebastian the goldsmith invariably replied, "At the feet of your grace, Don Luis."

He supped sparingly, and the last act of his day was his one act of luxury; his cup of chocolate or glass of *agraz*, according to season, at the Café de la Luna in the Plaza Mayor. This was his title to table and chair, and the respect of all Valladolid from dusk until nine—on the last stroke of which, saluting the company, who rose almost to a man, he retired to his garret and thin bed.

Pepe, the head waiter at the Luna, who had been there for thirty years, Gomez the barber, who was sixty-three and looked forty, Sebastian the goldsmith, well over middle age, and the old priest of Las Angustias, who had confessed him every Friday and said mass at the same altar every morning since his ordination (God knows how long ago), would have testified to the fact that Don Luis had never once varied his daily habits within time of memory.

They would have been wrong, of course, like all clean sweepers; for in addition to his inheritance of ruin, misfortunes had graved him deeply. Valladolid knew it well. His wife had left him, his son had gone to the devil. He bore the first blow like a stoic, not moving a muscle nor varying a habit: the second sent him on a journey. The barber, the water-seller, Pepe the waiter, Sebastian the deft were troubled about him for a week or more. He came back, and hid his wound, speaking to no one of it; and no one dared to pity him. And although he resumed his routine and was outwardly the same man, we may trace to that last stroke of Fortune the wasted splendour of his eyes, the look of a dying stag, which, once seen, haunted the observer. He was extraordinarily handsome, except for his narrow shoulders and hollow eyes, flawlessly clean in person and dress; a tall, straight, hawk-nosed, sallow gentleman. The Archbishop of Toledo was his first cousin, a cadet of his house. He was entitled to wear his hat in the presence of the Queen, and he lived upon fivepence a day.

Manvers, reaching Valladolid in the evening, reposed himself for a day or two, and recovered from his shock. He saw the sights, conversed with affability with all and sundry, drank *agraz* in the Café de la Luna. He must have beamed without knowing it upon Don Luis, for his brisk appearance, twisted smile and abrupt manner were familiar to that watchful gentleman by the time that, sweeping aside the curtain like a buffet of wind, he entered the goldsmith's shop in the Plaza San Benito. He came in a little before twilight one afternoon, holding by a string in one hand some swinging object, taking off his hat with the other as soon as he was past the curtain of the door.

"Can you," he said to Sebastian, in very fair Spanish, "take up a job for me a little out of the common?" As he spoke he swung the object into the air, caught it and enclosed it with his hand. Don Luis, in a dark corner of the shop, sat back in his accustomed chair, and watched him. He sat very still, a picture of mournful interest, shrouding his mouth in his hand.

Sebastian, first master of his craft in a city of goldsmiths, was far too much the gentleman to imply that any command of his customer need not be extraordinary. Bowing with gravity, and adjusting the glasses upon his fine nose, he replied that when he understood the nature of the business he should be better instructed for his answer. Thereupon Manvers opened his hand and passed over the counter a brass crucifix.

It is difficult to disturb the self-possession of a gentleman of Spain; Sebastian did not betray by a twitch what his feelings or thoughts may have been. He gravely scrutinised the battered cross, back and front, was polite enough to ignore the greasy string, and handed it back without a single word. It may have been worth half a *real*; to watch his treatment of it was cheap at a dollar.

Manvers, however, flushed with annoyance, and spoke somewhat loftily. "Am I to understand that you will, or will not oblige me?"

Sebastian temperately replied, "You are to understand, señor caballero, that I am at your disposition, but also that I do not yet know what you wish me to do." Manvers laughed, and the air was clearer.

"A thousand pardons," he said, "a thousand pardons for my stupidity. I can tell you in two minutes what I want done with this thing." He held it in the flat of his hand, and looked from it to the jeweller, as he succinctly explained his wishes.

"I want you," he said, "to encase this cross completely, in thin gold plates." Conscious of Sebastian's portentous gravity, perhaps of Don Luis in his dark corner, he showed himself a little self-conscious also and added, "It's a curious desire of mine, I know, but there's a reason for it, which is neither here nor there. Make for me then," he went on, "of thin gold plates, a matrix to hold this cross. It must have a lid, also, which shall open upon hinges, here—" he indicated the precise points—"and close with a clasp, here. Let the string also be encased in gold. I don't know how you will do it—that is a matter for your skill; but I wish the string to remain where it is, intact, within a gold covering. This casing should be pliable, so that the cross could hang, if necessary, round the neck of a person—as it used to hang. Do I make myself understood?"

The Castilians are not a curious people, but this commission did undoubtedly interest Sebastian the jeweller. Professionally speaking, it was a delicate piece of work; humanly, could have but one explanation. So, at least, he judged.

What Don Luis may have thought of it, there's no telling. If you had watched him closely you would have seen the pupils of his eyes dilate, and then contract—just like those of a caged owl, when he becomes aware of a mouse circling round him.

But while Don Luis could be absorbed in the human problem, it was not so with his friend. Points of detail engaged him in a series of suggestions which threatened to be prolonged, and which maddened the Englishman. Was the outline of the cross to be maintained in the casing? Undoubtedly it was, otherwise you might as well hang a card-case round your neck! The hinges, now—might they not better be here, and here, than there, and there? Manvers was indifferent as to the hinges. The fastening? Let the fastening be one which could be snapped-to, and open upon a spring. The chain—ah, there was some nicety required for that. From his point of view, Sebastian said, with the light of enthusiasm irradiating his face, that that was the cream of the job.

Manvers, wishing to get out of the shop, begged him to do the best he could, and turned to go. At the door he stopped short and came back. There was one thing more. Inside the lid of the case, in the centre of the cross, he wished to have engraved the capital letter M, and below that a date—12 May, 1861. That was really all, except that he was staying at the Parador de las Diligencias, and would call in a week's time. He left his card—Mr. Osmund Manvers, Filcote Hall, Taunton; Oxford and Cambridge Club—elegantly engraved. And then he departed, with a jerky salute to Don Luis, grave in his corner.

That card, after many turns back and face, was handed to Don Luis for inspection, while Sebastian looked to him for light over the rim of his spectacles.

"M for Manvers," he said presently, since Don Luis returned the card without comment. "That is probable, I imagine."

"It is possible," said Don Luis with his grand air of indifference. "With an Englishman anything is possible."

Sebastian did not pretend to be indifferent. He hummed an air, and played it out with his fingers on the counter as he thought. Then he flashed into life. "The twelfth of May! That is just a week ago. I have it, Señor Don Luis! Hear my explanation. This thing of nought was presented to the gentleman upon his birthday—the twelfth of May. The giver was poor, or he would have made a more considerable present; and he was very dear to the gentleman, or he would not have dared to present such a thing. Nor

- 39 -

would the gentleman, I think, have treated it so handsomely. Handsomely!" He made a rapid calculation. "*Ah, que!* He is paying its weight in gold." Now—this was in his air of triumph—*now* what had Don Luis to say?

That weary but unbowed antagonist of hunger and despair, after shrugging his shoulders, considered the matter, while Sebastian waited. "Why do you suppose," he asked at length, "that the giver of this thing was a man?"

"I do not suppose it," cried Sebastian. "I never did suppose it. The cross has been worn"—he passed his finger over its smooth back—"and recently worn. Men do not carry such things about them, unless they are——"

"What this gentleman is," said Don Luis. "A woman gave him this. A wench."

Sebastian bowed, and with sparkling eyes re-adjusted his inferences.

"That being admitted, we are brought a little further. M does not stand for Manvers—for what gentleman would give himself the trouble to engrave his own name upon a cross? It is the initial of the giver's name—and observe. Señor Don Luis, he is very familiar with her, since he knows her but by one." He looked through his shop window to the light, as he began a catalogue. "Maria—Mariquita—Maritornes—Margarita—Mariana—Mercedes—Miguela——" He stopped short, and his eyes encountered those of his friend, fast upon him, ominous and absorbing. He showed a certain confusion. "Any one of these names, it might be, Señor Don Luis."

"Or Manuela," said the other, still regarding him steadily.

"Or Manuela—true," said Sebastian with a bow, and a perceptible deepening of colour.

"In any case——" Don Luis rose, removed a speck of dust from his *capa*, and adjusted his beaver—"In any case, my friend, we may assume the 12th of May to be our gentleman's birthday. *Adios, hermano.*"

Sebastian was about to utter his usual ceremonial assurance, when a thought drove it out of his head.

"Stay, stay a moment, Don Luis of my soul!" He snapped his fingers together in his excitement.

"*Ah, que!*" muttered Don Luis, who had his hand upon the latch.

"A birthday—what is it? A thing of every year. Is he likely to receive a brass crucifix worth two maravedis every year, and every year to sheathe it in gold? Never! This marks a solemnity—a great solemnity. Listen, I will tell you. It marks the end of a liaison. She has left him—but tenderly; or he has left her—but regretfully. It becomes a touching affair. Do you not agree with me?"

Don Luis raised his eyebrows. "I have no means of agreeing with you, Sebastian. It may mark the end of a story—or the beginning. Who knows?" He threw out his arms and let them drop. "Señor God, who cares?"

# CHAPTER X

## FURTHER EPISODES IN THE LIFE OF DON LUIS RAMONEZ

Goldsmithing is the art of Valladolid, and Sebastian was its master. That was the opinion of the mystery, and his own opinion. He never concealed it; but he had now to confess that Manvers had given him a task worthy of his powers. To cut out and rivet the links of the chain, which was to sheathe a piece of string and leave it all its pliancy—"I tell you, Don Luis of my soul," he said, peering up from his board, "there is no man in our mystery who could cope with it—and very few frail ladies who could be worthy of it." Don Luis added that there could be few young men who could be capable of commanding it; but Sebastian had now conceived an admiration for his client.

"Fantasia, vaya! The English have the hearts of poets in the bodies of beeves. Did your grace ever hear of Doña Juanita—who in the French war ran half over Andalusia in pursuit of an Englishman? I heard my father tell the tale. Not his person claimed her, but his heart of a poet. Well, he married her, and from camp to camp she trailed after him, while he helped our nation beat Bonaparte. But one day they received the hospitality of a certain hidalgo, and had removed many leagues from him by the next night, when they camped beside a river. Dinner was eaten in the tents, and dessert served up in a fine bowl. 'Sola!' says the Englishman, 'that bowl—it is not ours, my heart?' 'No,' says Juanita, 'it is the hidalgo's, and was packed with our furniture in the hurry of departing.' 'Por dios!' says the Englishman, 'it must be returned to him.' But how? He could not go himself, for at that moment there entered an alguazil with news of the enemy. What then? 'Juanita will go,' says the Englishman, and went out, buckling his sword. Señor Don Luis, she went, on horseback, all those leagues, beset with foes, in the night, and rendered back the bowl. I tell you, the hearts of poets!"

Don Luis, who had been nodding his high approval, now stared. "*Ah, que!* But the poet was Doña Juanita, it seems to me," he said.

"Pardon me, dear sir, not at all. Our Spanish ladies are not fond of travel. It was the Englishman who inspired her. He was a poet with a vision. In his vision he saw her going. Safely then, he could say, she will go, because he, to whom time was nothing, saw her in the act. He did not give directions—he went out to engage the enemy. Then she went—vaya!"

"You may be sure," Sebastian went on, "that my client is a poet and a fine fellow. You may be sure that the gift of this trifle has touched his heart. It was not given lightly. The measure of his care is the measure of its worth in his eyes."

Don Luis allowed the possibility, by raising his eyebrows and tilting his head sideways; a shrug with an accent, as it were. Then he allowed Sebastian to clinch his argument by saying that the Englishman seemed to be getting the better of his emotion; for here was a week, said he, and he had not once been into the shop to inquire for his relic. Sebastian was down upon the admission. "What did I tell you, my friend? Is not that the precise action of our Englishman who said, 'Juanita will ride,' and went out and left her at the table? Precisely the same! And Juanita rode—and I, by God, have wrought at the work he gave me to do, and finished it. Vaya, Don Luis, it is not amiss."

It had to be confessed that it was not; and Manvers calling one morning later was as warm in his praises as his Spanish and his temperament would admit. He paid the bill without demur.

Sebastian, though he was curious, was discreet. Don Luis, however, thought proper to remark upon the crucifix, when he chanced to meet its owner in the Church of Las Angustias.

That church contains a famous statue of Juan de Juni's, a *Mater dolorosa* most tragic and memorable. Manvers, in his week's prowling of the city, had come upon it by accident, and visited it more than once. She sits, Our Lady of Sorrows, upon a rock, in her widow's weeds, exhibiting a grief so intense that she may well have been made larger than life, in order to support a misery which would crush a mortal woman. It is so fine, this emblem of divine suffering, that it obscures its tawdry surroundings, its pinchbeck tabernacle, gilding and red paint. When she is carried in a *paso*, as whiles she is, no spangled robe is put over her, no priest's vestment, no crown or veil. Seven swords are driven into her bosom: she is unconscious of them. Her wounds are within; but they call her in Valladolid Señora de los Chuchillos.

It was in the presence of this august mourner that Manvers was found by Don Luis Ramonez after mass. He had been present at the ceremony, but not assisting, and had his crucifix open in the palm of his hand when the other rose from his knees and saw him.

After a moment's hesitation the old gentleman stayed till the worshippers had departed, and then drew near to Manvers, and bowed ceremoniously.

"You will forgive me for remarking upon what you have in your hand, señor caballero," he said, "when I tell you that I was present, not only at the commissioning of the work, but at its daily progress to the perfection it now bears. My friend, Don Sebastian, had every reason to be contented with his masterpiece. I am glad to learn from him that you were no less satisfied."

Manvers, who had immediately shut down his hand, now opened it. "Yes," he said, "it's a beautiful piece of work. I am more than pleased."

"It is a setting," said Don Luis, "which, in this country, we should give to a relic of the True Cross."

Manvers looked quickly up. "I know, I know. It must seem to you a piece of extravagance on my part——; but there were reasons, good reasons. I could hardly have done less."

Don Luis bowed gravely, but said nothing. Manvers felt impelled to further discussion. Had he been a Spaniard he would have left the matter where it was; but he was not, so he went awkwardly on.

"It's a queer story. For some reason or another I don't care to speak of it. The person who gave me this trinket did me—or intended me—an immense service, at a great cost."

"She too," said Don Luis, looking at the Dolorosa, "may have had her reasons."

"It was a woman," said Manvers, with quickening colour, "I see no harm in saying so. I was going to tell you that she believed herself indebted to me for some trifling attention I had been able to show her previously. That is how I explain her giving me the crucifix. It was her way of thanking me—a pretty way. I was touched."

Don Luis waved his hand. "It is very evident, señor caballero. Your way of recording it is exemplary: her way, perhaps, was no less so."

"You will think me of a sentimental race," Manvers laughed, "and I won't deny it—but it's a fact that I was touched."

Don Luis, who, throughout the conversation, had been turning the crucifix about, now examined the inscription. He held it up to the light that he might see it better. Manvers observed him, but did not take the hint which was thus, rather bluntly, conveyed him. The case once more in his breast-pocket, he saluted Don Luis and went his way.

Shortly afterwards he left Valladolid on horseback.

Perhaps a week went by, perhaps ten days; and then Don Luis had a visitor one night in the Café de la Luna, a mean-looking, pale and harassed visitor with a close-cropped head, whose eyebrows flickered like summer fires in the sky, who would not sit down, who kept his felt hat rolled in his hands, whose deference was extreme, and accepted as a matter of course. He was known in Valladolid, it seemed. Pepe knew him, called him Tormillo.

"A sus piés," was the burthen of his news so far, "a los piés de V$^d$, Señor Don Luis."

Don Luis took no sort of notice of him, but continued to smoke his cigarette. He allowed the man to stand shuffling about for some three minutes before he asked him what he wanted.

That was exactly what Tormillo found it so difficult to explain. His eyebrows ran up to hide in his hair, his hands crushed his hat into his chest. "Quien sabe?" he gasped to the company, and Don Luis drained his glass.

Then he looked at the man. "Well, Tormillo?"

Tormillo shifted his feet. "Ha!" he gasped, "who knows what the señores may be pleased to say? How am I to know? They ask for an interview, a short interview in the light of the moon. Two caballeros in the Campo Grande—ready to oblige your Excellency."

"And who, pray, are these caballeros? And why do they stand in the Campo?" Don Luis asked in his grandest manner. Tormillo wheedled in his explanations.

"That which they have to report, Señor Don Luis," he began, craning forward, whispering, grinning his extreme goodwill—"Oho! it is not matter for the Café. It is matter for the moon, and the shade of trees. And these caballeros——"

Don Luis paid the hovering Pepe his shot, rose and threw his cloak over his shoulder. "Follow me," he said, and, saluting the company, walked into the *plaza*. He crossed it, and entered a narrow street, where the overhanging houses make a perpetual shade. There he stopped. "Who are these gentlemen?" he said abruptly. Tormillo seemed to be swimming.

"Worthy men, Señor Don Luis, worthy of confidence. To me they said little; it is for your grace's ear. They have titles. They are written across their foreheads. It is not for me to speak. Who am I, Tormillo, but the slave of your nobility?"

The more he prevaricated, the less Don Luis pursued him. Stiffening his neck, shrouded in, his cloak, he now stalked stately from street to street until he came to the Puerta del Carmen, through the battlements of which the moon could be seen looking coldly upon Valladolid. He was known to the gatekeeper, who bowed, and opened for him the wicket.

The great space of the Campo Grande lay like a silver pool, traversed only by the thin shadows of the trees. At the farther end of the avenue, which leads directly from the gate, two men were standing close together. Beyond them a little were two horses, one snuffing at the bare earth, the other with his head thrown up, and ears pricked forward. Don Luis turned sharply on his follower.

"Guardia Civil?"

"Si, señor, si," whispered Tormillo, and his teeth clattered like castanets. Don Luis went on without faltering, and did not stay until he was within easy talking distance of the two men. Then it was that he threw up his head, with a fine gesture of race, and acknowledged the saluting pair. Tormillo, at this point, turned aside and stood miserably under a tree, wringing his hands.

"Good evening to you, friends. I am Don Luis Ramonez, at your service."

The pair looked at each other: presently one of them spoke.

"At the feet of Señor Don Luis."

"Your business is pressing, and secret?"

"Si, Señor Don Luis, pressing, and secret, and serious. We have to ask your grace to be prepared."

"I thank you. My preparations are made already. Present your report."

He took a cigarette from his pocket, and lit it with a steady hand. The flame of the match showed his brows and deep-set eyes. If ever a man had acquaintance with grief printed upon him, it was he. But throughout the interview the glowing weed could be seen, a waxing and waning rim of fire, lighting up his grey moustache and then hovering in mid-air, motionless.

The officer appointed to speak presented his report in these terms.

"We were upon our round about the wood of La Huerca six days ago, and had occasion to visit the Convent of La Peña. Upon information received from the Prior we questioned a certain religious, who admitted that he had recently buried a man in the wood. After some hesitation, which we had the means of overcoming, he conducted us to the grave. We disinterred the deceased, who had been murdered. Señor Don Luis——"

"Proceed," said Don Luis coldly. "I am listening."

"Sir," said the officer. "It was the body of a young man who had come from Pobledo. He called himself Estéban Vincaz." Tormillo, under his tree across the avenue, howled and rent himself. Don Luis heard him.

"Precisely," he said to the officer. "Have the goodness to wait while I silence that dog over there." He went rapidly over the roadway to Tormillo, grasped him by the shoulder and spoke to him in a vehement whisper. That was the single action by which he betrayed himself. He returned to his interview.

"I am now at leisure again. Let us resume our conversation. You questioned the religious, you say? When did the assassination take place?"

"Don Luis, it was upon the twelfth of May."

"Ah," said Don Luis, "the twelfth of May? And did he know who committed it?"

"Señor Don Luis, it was a woman."

The wasted eyes were upon the speaker, and made him nervous. He turned away his head. But Don Luis continued his cross-examination.

"She was a fair woman, I believe? A Valencian?"

"Señor, si," said the man. "Fair and false, a Valencian."

Of Valencia they say, "*La carne es herba, la herba agua, el hombre muger, la muger nada.*"

"Her name," said Don Luis, "began with M."

"Señor, si. It was Manuela, the dancing girl—called La Valenciana, La Fierita, and a dozen other things. But, pardon me the liberty, your worship had been informed?"

"I knew something," said Don Luis, "and suspected something. I am much obliged to you, my friends. Justice will be done. Good night to you." He turned, touching the brim of his hat; but the man went after him.

"A thousand pardons, señor Don Luis, but we have our duty to the State."

"Eh!" said Don Luis sharply. "Well, then, you had best set to work upon it."

"If your worship has any knowledge of the whereabouts of this woman——"

"I have none," said Don Luis. "If I had I would impart it, and when I have it shall be yours. Go now with God."

He crossed the pathway of light, laid his hand on the shoulder of the weeping Tormillo. "Come, I need you," he said. Tormillo crept after him to his lodging, and the Guardias Civiles made themselves cigarettes.

The following day a miracle was reported in Valladolid. Don Luis Ramonez was not in his place in the Café de la Luna. Sebastian the goldsmith, Gomez the pert barber, Pepe the waiter, Micael the water-seller of the Plaza Mayor knew nothing of his whereabouts. The old priest of Las Angustias might have told if his lips had not been sealed. But in the course of the next morning it was noised about that his Worship had left the city for Madrid, accompanied by a servant.

# CHAPTER XI

## GIL PEREZ DE SEGOVIA

Before he left Valladolid Manvers had sold his horse for what he could get, and had taken the *diligencia* as far as Segovia. Not a restful conveyance, the *diligencia* of Spain: therefore, in that wonderful city of towers, silence, and guarded windows, he stayed a full week, in order, as he put it, that his bones might have time to set.

THE TOWERS OF SEGOVIA.

**The towers of Segovia.**

There it was that he became the property of Gil Perez, who met him one day on the doorstep of his hotel, saluted him with a flourish and said in dashing English, "Good morning, Mister. I am the man for you. I espeak English very good, Dutch, what you like. I show you my city; you pleased—eh?" He had a merry brown face, half of a quiz and half of a rogue, was well-dressed in black, wore his hat, which was now in his hand, rather over one ear. Manvers met his saucy eyes for a minute, saw anxiety behind their impudence, could not be angry, burst into a laugh, and was heartily joined by Gil Perez.

"That very good," said Gil. "You laugh, I very glad. That tell me is all right." He immediately became serious. "I serve you well, sir, there's no mistake. I am Gil Perez, too well known to the landlord of this hotel. You see?" He showed his teeth, which were excellent, and he had also, Manvers reflected, shown his hand, for what it was worth—which argued a certain security.

"Gil Perez," he said, on an impulse, "I shall take you at your word. Do you wait where you are." He turned back into the inn and sought his landlord, who was smoking a cigar in the kitchen while the maids bustled about. From him he learned what there was to be known of Gil Perez; that he was a native of Cadiz who had been valet to an English officer at Gibraltar, followed him out to the Crimea, nursed him through dysentery (of which he had died), and had then begged his way home again to Spain. He had been in Segovia a year or two, acting as guide or interpreter when he could, living on nothing a day mostly and doing pretty well on it.

"He has been in prison, I shall not conceal from your honour," said the landlord. "He stabbed a man under the ribs because he had insulted the English. Gil Perez loves your nation. He considers you to be the natural protectors of the poor. He will serve you well, you may be sure."

"That's what he told me himself," said Manvers.

The landlord rested his eyes—large, brown and solemn as those of an ox—upon his guest. "He told you the truth, señor. He will serve you better than he would serve me. You will be his god."

"I hope not," said Manvers, and went out to the door again. Gil Perez, who had been smoking out in the sun, threw his *papelito* away, stood at attention and saluted smartly.

"What was the name of your English master?" Manvers asked him. Gil replied at once.

"'E call Capitan Rodney. Royalorse Artillery. 'E say 'Gunner.' 'E was a gentleman, sir."

"I'm sure he was," said Manvers.

"My master espeak very good Espanish. 'E say 'damn your eyes' all the time; and call me 'Little devil' just the same. Ah," said Gil Perez, shaking his head. "'E very good gentleman to me, sir—good master. I loved 'im. 'E dead." For a minute he gazed wistfully at the sky; then, as if to clinch the sad matter, he turned to Manvers. "I bury 'im all right," he said briskly, and nodded inward the fact.

Manvers considered for a moment. "I'll give you," he said, and looked at Gil keenly as he said it, "I'll give you one *peseta* a day." He saw his eyes fade and grow blank, though the genial smile hovered still on his lips. Then the light broke out upon him again.

"All right, sir," he said. "I take, and thank you very much."

Manvers said immediately, "I'll give you two," and Gil Perez accepted the correction silently, with a bow. By the end of the day they were on the footing of friends, but not without one short crossing of swords. After dinner, when Manvers strolled to the door of the inn, he found his guide waiting for him. Gil was in a confidential humour, it seemed.

"You care see something, sir?"

"What sort of a thing, for instance?" he was asked.

Gil Perez shrugged. "What you like, sir." He peered into his patron's face, and there was infinite suggestion in his next question. "You see fine women?"

Manvers had expected something of the sort and had a steely stare ready for him. "No, thanks," he said drily, and Gil saluted and withdrew. He was at the door next morning, affable yet respectful, confident in his powers of pleasing, of interesting, of arranging everything; but he never presumed again. He knew his affair.

Three days' sightseeing taught master and man their bearings. Manvers got into the way of forgetting that Gil Perez was there, except when it was convenient to remember him; Gil, on his part, learned to distinguish between his patron's soliloquies and his conversation. He never made a mistake after the third day. If Manvers, in the course of a ramble, stopped abruptly, buried a hand in his beard and said aloud that he would be shot if he knew which way to turn, Gil Perez watched him closely, but made no remark.

Even, "Look here, you know, this won't do," failed to move him beyond a state of tension, like that of a cat in the act to pounce. He had found out that Manvers talked to himself, and was put about by interruptions; and if you realise how sure and certain he was that he knew much better than his master what was the very thing, or the last thing, he ought to do, you will see that he must have put considerable restraint upon himself.

But loyalty was his supreme virtue. From the moment Manvers had taken him on at two pesetas a day he became the perfect servant of a perfect master. He could have no doubt, naturally, of his ability to serve— his belief in himself never wavered; but he had none either in his gentleman's right to command. I believe if Manvers had desired him to cut off his right hand he would have complied with a smile. "Very good, master. You wanta my 'and? I do."

If he had a failing it was this: nothing on earth would induce him to talk his own language to his master. He was unmoved by encouragement, unconvinced by the fluency of Manvers' Castilian periods; he would have risked his place upon this one point of honour.

"Espanish no good, sir, for you an' me," he said once with an irresistible smile. "Too damsilly for you. Capitan Rodney, 'e teach, me Englisha speech. Now I know it too much. No, sir. You know what they say—them *filosofistas*?" he asked him on another encounter. "They say, God Almighty 'e maka this world in Latin—ver' fine for thata big job. Whata come next? Adamo 'e love his lady in Espanish—esplendid for maka women love. That old Snaka 'e speak to 'er in French—that persuade 'er too much. Then Eva she esplain in Italian—ver' soft espeech. Adamo 'e say, That all righta. Then God Almighty ver' savage. 'E turn roun' on them two. 'E say, That be blowed, 'e say in English. They understan' 'im too much. Believe me—is the best for you an' me, sir. All people understan' that espeech."

Taken as a guide, he installed himself as body servant, silently, tactfully, but infallibly. Manvers caught him one morning putting boots by his door. "Hulloa, Gil Perez," he called out, "what are you doing with my boots?"

Gil's confidential manner was a thing to drink. "That *mozo*, master—'e fool. 'E no maka shine. I show him how Capitan Rodney lika 'is boots. See 'is a face in 'em." He smirked at his own as he spoke, and was so pleased that Manvers said no more.

The same night he stood behind his master's chair. Manvers contented himself by staring at him. Gil Perez smiled with his bright eyes and became exceedingly busy. Manvers continued to stare, and presently Gil Perez was observed to be sweating. The poor fellow was self-conscious for once in his life. Obliged to justify himself, he leaned to his master's ear.

"That *mozo*, sir, too much of a dam fool. Imposs' you estand 'im. I tell 'im, This gentleman no like garlic down his neck. I say, You breathe too 'ard, my fellow—too much garlic. This gentleman say, Crikey, what a stink! That no good."

There was no comparison between the new service and the old; and so it was throughout. Gil Perez drove out the chambermaid and made Manvers' bed; he brushed his clothes as well as his boots, changed his linen for him, saw to the wash—in fine, he made himself indispensable. But when Manvers announced his coming departure, there was a short tussle, preceded by a pause for breath.

Gil Perez inquired of the sky, searched up the street, searched down. A group of brown urchins hovered, as always, about the stranger, ready to risk any deadly sin for the chance of a maravedi or the stump of a cigar.

Gil snatched at one by the bare shoulder and spoke him burning words. "*Canalla*," he cried him, "horrible flea! Thou makest the air to reek—impossible to breathe. Fly, thou gnat of the midden, or I crack thee on my thumb."

The boys retired swearing, and Gil, with desperate calling-up of reserves, faced his ordeal. "Ver' good, master, we go when you like. We see Escorial—fine place—see La Granja, come by Madrid thata way. I get 'orses 'ow you please." Then he had an inspiration, and beamed all over his face. "Or mules! We 'ave mules. Mules cheap, 'orses dear too much in Segovia."

Manvers could see very well what he was driving at. "I think I'll take the *diligencia*, Gil Perez."

Gil shrugged. "'Ow you like, master. Fine air, thata way. Ver' cheap way to go. You take my advice, you go *coupé*. I go *redonda* more cheap. Give me your passport, master—I take our place."

"Yes, I know," said Manvers. "But I'm not sure that I need take you on with me. I travel without a servant mostly."

Gil grappled with his task. He dropped his air of assumption; his eyes glittered.

"I save you money, master. You find me good servant—make a difference, yes?"

"Oh, a great deal of difference," Manvers admitted. "I like you; you suit me excellently well, but——" He considered what he had to do in Madrid, and frowned over it. Manuela was there, and he wished to see Manuela. He had not calculated upon having a servant when he had promised himself another interview with her, and was not at all sure that he wanted one. On the other hand, Gil might be useful in a number of ways— and his discretion and tact were proved. While he hesitated, Gil Perez saw his opportunity and darted in.

"I know Madrid too much," he said. "All the ways, all the peoples I know. Imposs' you live 'appy in Madrid withouta me." He smiled all over his face—and when he did that he was irresistible. "You try," he concluded, just like a child.

Manvers, on an impulse, drew from his pocket the gold-set crucifix. "Look at that, Gil Perez," he said, and put it in his hands.

Gil looked gravely at it, hack and front. He nodded his approval. "Pretty thing——" and he decided off-hand. "In Valladolid they make."

"Open it," said Manvers; but it was opened, before he had spoken. Gil's eyes widened, while the pupils of them contracted intensely. He read the inscription, pondered it; to the crucifix itself he gave but a momentary glance. Then he shut the case and handed it back to his master.

"I find 'er for you," he said soberly; and that settled it.

# CHAPTER XII

## A GLIMPSE OF MANUELA

Gil Perez had listened gravely to the tale which his master told him. He nodded once or twice, and asked a few questions in the course of the narrative—questions of which Manvers could not immediately see the bearing. One was concerned with her appearance. Did she wear rings in her ears? He had to confess that he had not observed. Another was interjected when he described how she had grown stiff under his arm when Estéban drew alongside.

Gil had nodded rapidly, and became impatient as Manvers insisted on the fact. "Of course, of course!" he had said, and then he asked, Did she stiffen her arm and point the first and last fingers of it, keeping the middle pair clenched?

Manvers understood him, and replied that he had not noticed any such thing, but that he did not believe she feared the Evil Eye. He went on with his story uninterrupted until the climax. He had found the crucifix, he said, on his return from bathing, and had been pleased with her for leaving it. Then he related the discovery of the body and his talk with Fray Juan de la Cruz. Here came in Gil's third question. "Did she return your handkerchief?" he asked—and sharply.

Manvers started. "By George, she never did!" he exclaimed. "And I don't wonder at it," he said on reflection. "If she had to knife that fellow, and confess to Fray Juan, and escape for her life, she had enough to do. Of course, she may have left it in the wood."

Gil Perez pressed his lips together. "She got it still," he said. "We find 'er—I know where to look for it."

If he did he kept his knowledge to himself, though he spoke freely enough of Manuela on the way to Madrid.

"This Manuela," he explained, "is a Valenciana—where you find fair women with black men. Valencianos like Moors—love too much white women. I think Manuela is not Gitanilla; she is what you call a Alfanalf. Then she is like the Gitanas, as proud as a fire, but all the same a Christian—make free with herself. A Gitana never dare love Christian man—imposs' she do that. Sometimes all the same she do it. I think Manuela made like that."

Committed to the statement, he presently saw a cheerful solution of it. "Soon see!" he added, and considered other problems. "That dead man follow Manuela to kill 'er," he decided. "When 'e find 'er with you, master, 'e say, 'Now I know why you run, *hija de perra*. Now I kill two and get a 'orse.' You see?"

"Yes," said Manvers, "I see that. And you think that he told her what he meant to do?"

"Of course 'e tell," said Gil Perez with scorn. "Make it too bad for 'er. Make 'er feel sick."

"Brute!" cried Manvers; but Gil went blandly on.

"'E 'ate 'er so much that 'e feel 'ungry and thirsty. 'E eat before 'e kill. Must do it—too 'ungry. Then she go near 'im, twisting 'erself about— showing 'erself to please him. 'You kiss me, my 'eart,' she say; 'I love you all the same. Kiss me—then you kill.' 'E look at 'er—she very fine girl—give pleasure to see. 'E think, 'I love 'er first—strangle after'—and go on looking. She 'old 'im fast and drag down 'is 'ead—all the time she know where 'e keep *navaja*. She cling and kiss—then nip out *navaja*, and *click*! 'E dead man." Enthusiasm burned in his black eyes, he stood cheering in his stirrups. "Señor Don Dios! that very fine! I give twenty dollars to see 'er make 'im love."

Manvers for his part, grew the colder as his man waxed warm. He was clear, however, that he must find the girl and protect her from any trouble that might ensue. She had put herself within the law to save him from the knife; she must certainly be defended from the perils of the law.

From what he could learn of Spanish justice that meant money and influence. These she should have; but there should be no more pastorals. Her kisses had been sweet, the aftertaste was sour in the mouth. Gil Perez with his eloquence and dramatic fire had cured him of hankering after more of them. The girl was a rip, and there was an end of it.

He did not blame himself in the least for having kissed a rip—once. There was nothing in that. But he had kissed her twice—and that second kiss had given significance to the first. To think of it made him sore all over; it implied a tender relation, it made him seem the girl's lover. Why, it almost justified that sick-faced, grinning rascal, whose staring eyes had shocked him out of his senses. And what a damned fool he had made of himself with the crucifix! He ground his teeth together as he cursed himself for a sentimental idiot.

For the rest of the way it was Gil Perez who cried up the quest—until he was curtly told by his master to talk about something else; and then Gil could have bitten his tongue off for saying a word too much.

A couple of days at the Escorial, with nothing of Manuela to interfere, served Manvers to recover his tone. Before he was in the capital he was again that good and happy traveller, to whom all things come well in their seasons, to whom the seasons of all things are the seasons at which they come. He liked the bustle and flaunt of Madrid, he liked its brazen front, its crowded *carreras*, and appetite for shows. There was hardly a day when the windows of the Puerta del Sol had not carpets on their balconies. Files of halberdiers went daily to and from the Palace and the Atocha, escorting some gilded, swinging coach; and every time the Madrileños serried and craned their heads. "*Viva Isabella!*" "*Abajo Don Carlos!*" or sometimes the other way about, the cries went up. Politics buzzed all about the square in the mornings; evening brimmed the cafés.

Manvers resumed his soul, became again the amused observer. Gil Perez bided his time, and contented himself with being the perfect body-servant, which he undoubtedly was.

On the first Sunday after arrival, without any order, he laid before his master a ticket for the *corrida*, such a one as comported with his dignity; but not until he was sure of his ground did he presume to discuss the gory spectacle. Then, at dinner, he discovered that Manvers had been more interested in the spectators than the fray, and allowed himself free discourse. The Queen and the Court, the *alcalde* and the Prime Minister, the *manolos* and *manolas*—he had plenty to say, and to leave unsaid. He just glanced at the performers—impossible to omit the *espada*—Corchuelo, the first in Spain. But the fastidious in Manvers was awake and edgy. He had not liked the bull-fight; so Gil Perez kept out of the arena. "I see one very grand old gentleman there, master," was one of his chance casts. "You see 'im? 'E grandee of Espain, too much poor, proud all the same. Put 'is 'at on so soon the Queen come in—Don Luis Ramonez de Alavia."

"Who's he?" asked Manvers.

"Great gentleman of Valladolid," said Gil Perez. "Grandee of Espain—no money—only pride." He did not add, as he might, that he had seen Manuela, or was pretty sure that he had. That was delicate ground.

But Manvers, who had forgotten all about her, went cheerfully his ways, and amused himself in his desultory fashion. After the close-pent streets of Segovia, where the wayfarer seems throttled by the houses, and one looks up for light and pants towards the stars and the air, he was pleased by the breadth of Madrid. The Puerto del Sol was magnificent—

like a lake; the Alcalá and San Geronimo were noble rivers, feeding it. He liked them at dawn when the hose-pipe had been newly at work and these great spaces of emptiness lay gleaming in the mild sunlight, exhaling freshness like that of dewy lawns. When, under the glare of noon, they lay slumbrous, they were impressive by their prodigality of width and scope; in the bustle and hum of dusk, with the cafés filling, and spilling over on to the pavements, he could not tire of them; but at night, the mystery of their magic enthralled him. How could one sleep in such a city? The Puerto del Sol was then a sea of dark fringed with shores of bright light. The two huge feeders of it—with what argosies they teemed! Shrouded craft!

MADRID BY NIGHT.

## Madrid by night.

That touch of the East, which you can never miss in Spain, wherever you may be, was unmistakable in Madrid, in spite of Court and commerce, in spite of newspaper, Stock Exchange, or Cortes. The cloaked figures moved silently, swiftly, seldom in pairs, without speech, with footfall scarcely audible. Now and again Manvers heard the throb of a guitar, now and again, with sudden clamour, the clack of castanets. But such noises stopped on the instant, and the traffic was resumed—whatever it was—secret, swift, impenetrable business.

For the most part this traffic of the night was conducted by men—young or old, as may be. The *capa* hid them all, kept their semblance as secret as their affairs. Here and there, but rarely, walked a woman, superbly, as Spanish women will, with a self-sufficiency almost arrogantly strong, robed in white, hooded with a white veil. The mantilla came streaming from the comb, swathed her pale cheeks and enhanced her lustrous eyes; but from top to toe she was (whatever else; she may have been, and it was not difficult to guess) in white.

Manvers watched them pass and repass; at a distance they looked like moths, but close at hand showed the carriage and intolerance of queens. They looked at him fairly as they passed, unashamed and unconcerned. Their eyes asked nothing from him, their lips wooed him not. There was none of the invitation such women extend elsewhere; far otherwise, it was the men who craved, the women who dispensed. When they listened it was as to a petitioner on his knees, when they gave it was like an alms. Imperious, free-moving, high-headed creatures, they interested him deeply.

It was true, as Gil Perez was quick to see, that at his first bull-fight Manvers had been unmoved by the actors, but stirred to the deeps by the spectators; if he had cared to see another it would have been to explore the secrets of this wonderful people, who could become animals without ceasing to be men and women. But why jostle on a bench, why endure the dust and glare of a *corrida* when you can see what Madrid can show you: the women by the Manzanares, or the nightly dramas of the streets?

Love in Spain, he began to learn, is a terrible thing; a grim tussle of wills, a matter of life and death, of meat and drink. He saw lovers, still as death, with upturned faces, tense and white, eating the iron of guarded balconies. Hour by hour they would stand there, waiting, watching, hoping on. No one interfered, no one remarked them. He heard a woman wail for her lover—wail and rock herself about, careless of who saw or heard her, and indeed neither seen nor heard. Once he saw a couple close together, vehement speech between them. A lovers' quarrel, terrible affair! The words seemed to scald. The man had had his say, and now it was her turn. He listened to her, touched but not persuaded—had his reasons, no doubt. But she! Manvers had not believed the heart of a girl could hold such a gamut of emotions. She was young, slim, very pale; her face was as white as her robe. But her eyes were like burning lakes; and her voice, hoarse though she had made herself, had a cry in it as sharp as a violin's, to out the very soul of you. She spoke with her hands too, with her shoulders and bosom, with her head and stamping foot. She never faltered though she ran from scorn of him to deep scorn of herself, and appealed in turn to his pride, his pity, his honour and his lust. She had no reticence, set no bounds: she was everything, or nothing; he was a god, or dirt of the kennel. In the end—and what a climax!—she stopped in the middle of a sentence, covered her eyes, sobbed, gave a broken cry, turned and fled away.

The man, left alone, spread his arms out, and lifted his face to the sky, as if appealing for the compassion of Heaven. Manvers could see by the light of a lamp which fell upon him that there were tears in his eyes. He was pitying himself deeply. "Señor Jesu, have pity!" Manvers heard him saying. "What could I do? Woe upon me, what could I do?"

To him there, as he stood wavering, returned suddenly the girl. As swiftly as she had gone she came back, like a white squall. "Ah, son of a thief? Ah, son of a dog!" and she struck him down with a knife over the shoulder-blade. He gasped, groaned, and dropped; and she was upon his breast in a minute, moaning her pity and love. She stroked his face, crooned over him, lavished the loveliest vocables of her tongue upon his worthless carcase, and won him by the very excess of her passion. The fallen man turned in her arms, and met her lips with his.

Manvers, shaking with excitement, left them. Here again was a Manuela! Manuela, her burnt face on fire, her eyes blown fierce by rage, her tawny hair streaming in the wind; Manuela with a knife, hacking the life out of Estéban, came vividly before him. Ah, those soft lips of hers could bare the teeth; within an hour of his kissing her she must have bared them, when she snarled on that other. And her eyes which had peered into his, to see if liking were there—how had they gleamed. upon the man she slew? Her sleekness then was that of the cat; but she had had no claws for him.

Why had she left him her crucifix? After all, had she murdered the fellow, or protected herself? She told the monk that she had been driven into a corner—to save Manvers and herself. Was he to believe that—or his own eyes? His eyes had just seen a Spanish girl with her lover, and his judgment was warped. Manuela might be of that sort—she had not been so to him. Nor could she ever be so, since there was no question of love between them now, and never could be.

"Come now," thus he reasoned with himself. "Come now, let us be reasonable." He had pulled her out of a scuffle and she had been grateful; she was pretty, he had kissed her. She was grateful, and had knifed a man who meant him mischief—and she had left him a crucifix.

Gratitude again. What had her gipsy skin and red kerchief to do with her heart and conscience? "Beware, my son, of the pathetic fallacy," he told himself, and as he turned into the carrera San Geronimo, beheld Manuela robed in white pass along the street.

He knew her immediately, though her face had but flashed upon him, and there was not a stitch upon her to remind him of the ragged creature of the plain. A white mantilla covered her hair, a white gown hid her to the ankles. He had a glimpse of a white stocking, and remarked her high-heeled white slippers. Startling transformation! But she walked like a free-moving creature of the open, and breasted the hot night as if she had been speeding through a woodland way. That was Manuela, who had lulled a man to save him.

After a moment or so of hesitation he followed her, keeping his distance. She walked steadily up the *carrera*, looking neither to right nor to left. Many remarked her, some tried to stop her. A soldier followed her pertinaciously, till presently she turned upon him in splendid rage and bade him be off.

Manvers praised her for that, and, quickening, gained upon her. She turned up a narrow street on the right. It was empty. Manvers, gaining rapidly, drew up level. They were now walking abreast, with only the street-way between them; but she kept a rigid profile to him—as severe, as proud and fine as the Arethusa's on a coin of Syracuse. The resemblance was striking; straight nose, short lip, rounded chin; the strong throat; unwinking eyes looking straight before her; and adding to these beauties of contour her splendid colouring, and carriage of a young goddess, it is not too much to say that Manvers was dazzled.

It is true; he was confounded by the excess of her beauty and by his knowledge of her condition. His experiences of life and cities could give him no parallel; but they could and did give him a dangerous sense of power. This glowing, salient creature was for him, if he would. One word, and she was at his feet.

For a moment, as he walked nearly abreast of her, he was ready to throw everything that was natural to him to the winds. She stirred a depth in him which he had known nothing of. He felt himself trembling all over—but while he hesitated a quick step behind caused him to look round. He saw a man following Manuela, and presently knew that it was Gil Perez.

And Gil, with none of his own caution, walked on her side of the street and, overtaking her, took off his hat and accosted her by some name which caused her to turn like a beast at bay. Nothing abashed, Gil asked her a question which clapped a hand to her side and sent her cowering to the wall. She leaned panting there while he talked rapidly, explaining with suavity and point. It was very interesting to Manvers to watch these two together, to see, for instance, how Gil Perez comported himself out of his master's presence; or how Manuela dealt with one of her own nation. They became strangers to him, people he had never known. He felt a foreigner indeed.

The greatest courtesy was observed, the most exact distance. Gil Perez kept his hat in his hand, his body at a deferential angle. His weaving hands were never still. Manuela, her first act of royal rage ended, held herself superbly. Her eyes were half closed, her lips tightly so; and she so contrived as to get the effect of looking down upon him from a height. Manvers imagined that his name or person was being brought into play, for once Manuela looked at her companion and bowed her head gravely. Gil Perez ran on with his explanations, and apparently convinced her judgment, for she seemed to consent to something which he asked of her; and presently walked on her way with a high head, while Gil Perez, still holding his hat, and still explaining, walked with her, but a little way behind her.

A cooling experience. Manvers strolled back to his hotel and his bed, with his unsuspected nature deeply hidden again out of sight. He wondered whether Gil Perez would have anything to tell him in the morning, or whether, on the other hand, he would be discreetly silent as to the adventure. He wondered next where that adventure would end. He had no reason to suppose his servant a man of refined sensibilities. Remembering his eloquence on the road to Madrid, the paean he blew upon the fairness of Valencian women, he laughed. "Here's a muddy wash upon my blood-boltered pastoral," he said aloud. "Here's an end of my knight-errantry indeed!"

There was nearly an end of him—for almost at the same moment he was conscious of a light step behind him and of a sharp stinging pain and a blow in the back. He turned wildly round and struck out with his stick. A man, doubled in two, ran like a hare down the empty street and vanished into the dark. Manvers, feeling sick and faint, leaned to recover himself against a doorway, and probably fell; for when he came to himself he was in his bed in the hotel, with Gil Perez and a grave gentleman in black standing beside him.

# CHAPTER XIII

## CHIVALRY OF GIL PEREZ

He felt stiff and stupid, with a roasting spot in his back between his shoulders; but he was able to see the light in Gil Perez' eyes—which was a good light, saying, "Well so far—but I look for more." Neither Gil nor the spectacled gentleman in black—the surgeon, he presumed—spoke to him, and disinclined for speech himself, Manvers lay watching their tip-toe ministrations, with spells of comfortable dozing in between, in the course of which he again lost touch with the world of Spain.

When he came to once more he was much better and felt hungry. He saw Gil Perez by the window, reading a little book. The sun-blinds were down to darken the room; Gil held his book slantwise to a chink and read diligently, moving his lips to pronounce the words.

"Gil Perez," said Manvers, "what are you reading?" Gil jumped up at once.

"You better, sir? Praised be God! I read," he said, "a little catholic book which calls itself 'The Garden of the Soul'—ver' good little book. What you call ver' 'ealthy—ver' good for 'im. But you are better, master. You 'ungry—I get you a broth." Which he did, having it hot and hot in the next room.

"Now I tell you all the 'istory of this affair," he said. "Last night I see Manuela out a walking. I follow 'er too much—salute 'er—she lift 'er 'ead back to strike me dead. I say, 'Señorita, one word. Why you give your crucifix to my master—ha?' Sir, she began to shake—'ead shake, knee shake; I think she fall into 'erself. You see flowers in frost all estiff, stand up all right. By'nbye the sun, 'e climb the sky—thosa flowers they fall esquash—all rotten insida. So Manuela fall into 'erself. Then I talk to 'er— she tell me all the 'istory of thata time. She kill Estéban Vincaz, she tell me—kill 'im quick, just what I told you. Becausa why? Becausa she dicksure Estéban kill you. But I say to 'er, Manuela, that was too bad, lady. Kill Estéban all the same. Ver' good for 'im, send 'im what you call kingdom-come like a shot. But you leava that crucifix on my master's plate—make 'im tender, too sorry for you. He think, Thata nice girl, very. I like 'er too much. Now 'e 'as your crucifix in gold, lika piece of Vera Cruz, lika Santa Teresa's finger, and all the world know you kill Estéban Vincaz and 'e like you. Sir, I make 'er sorry—she begin to cry. I think—" and Gil Perez walked to the window—"I think Manuela ver' fine girl—like a rose. Now, master—" and he returned to the bed—"I tell you something. That man who estab you las' night was Tormillo. You know who?"

Manvers shook his head. "Never heard of him, my friend. Who is he?"

"He is servant to Don Luis Ramonez, the same I see at the *corrida*. I tell you about 'im—no money, all pride."

Manvers stared. "And will you have the goodness to tell me why Don Luis should want to have me stabbed?"

"I tell you, sir," said Gil Perez. "Estéban Vincaz was Don Bartolomé Ramonez, son to Don Luis. Bad son 'e was, if you like, sir. Wil' oats, what you call. All the sama nobleman, all the sama only son to Don Luis."

Manvers considered this oracle with what light he had. "Don Luis supposes that I killed his son, then," he said. "Is that it?"

"'E damsure," said Gil Perez, blinking fast.

"On Manuela's account—eh?"

"Like a shot!" cried Gil Perez with enthusiasm.

"So of course he thinks it his duty to kill me in return."

"Of course 'e does, sir," said Gil. "I tell you, 'e is proud like the devil."

"I understand you," said Manvers. "But why does he hire a servant to do his revenges?"

"Because 'e think you dog," Gil replied calmly. "'E not beara touch you witha poker."

Manvers laughed, and said, "We'll leave it at that. Now I want to know one more thing. How on earth did Don Luis find out that I was in the wood with Manuela and his son?"

"Ah," said Gil Perez, "now you aska me something. Who knows?" He shrugged profusely. Then his face cleared. "Leave it to me, sir. I ask Tormillo." He was on his feet, as if about to find the assassin there and then.

"Stop a bit," said Manvers, "stop a bit, Gil. Now I must tell you that I also saw Manuela last night."

"Ah," said Gil Perez softly; and his eyes glittered.

"I saw her in the street," Manvers continued, watching his servant. "She was all in white."

Gil Perez blinked this fact. "Yes, sir," he said. "That is true. Poor girl." His eyes clouded over. "Poor Manuela!" he was heard to say to himself.

"I followed her for a while," said Manvers, "and saw you catch her up, and stop her. Then I went away; and then that rascal struck me in the back. Now do you suppose that Don Luis means to serve Manuela the same way?"

Gil Perez did not blink any more. "I think 'e wisha that," he said; "but I think 'e won't."

"Why not?"

"Because I tell Manuela what I see at the *corrida*. She was there too. She know it already. Bless you, she don't care."

"But I care," said Manvers sharply. "I've got her on my conscience. I don't intend her to suffer on my account."

"That," said Gil Perez, "is what she wanta do." He looked piercingly at his master. "You know, sir, I ask 'er for your 'andkerchief."

"Well?" Manvers raised his eyebrows.

"I tell you whata she do. She look allaways in the dark. Nobody there. Then she open 'er gown—so!" and Gil held apart the bosom of his shirt. "I see it in there." There were tears in Gil's eyes. "Poor Manuela!" he murmured, as if that helped him. "I make 'er give it me. No good she keepa that in there."

"Where is it?" he was asked. He tried to be his jaunty self, but failed.

"Not 'ere, sir. I 'ave it—I senda to the wash." Manvers looked keenly at him, but said nothing. He had a suspicion that Gil Perez was telling a lie.

"You had better get her out of Madrid," he said, after a while. "There may be trouble. Let her go and hide herself somewhere until this has blown over. Give me my pocket-book." He took a couple of bills out and handed them to Gil. "There's a hundred for her. Get her into some safe place—and the sooner the better. We'll see her through this business somehow."

Gil Perez—very unlike himself—suddenly snatched at his hand and kissed it. Then he sprang to his feet again and tried to look as if he had never done such a thing. He went to the door and put his head out, listening. "Doctor coming," he said. "All righta leave you with 'im."

"Of course it's all right," said Manvers. But Gil shook his head.

"Don Luis make me sick," he said. "No use 'e come 'ere."

"You mean that he might have another shot at me?"

Gil nodded; very wide-eyed and serious he was. "'E try. I know 'im too much." Manvers shut his eyes.

"I expect he'll have the decency to wait till I'm about again. Anyhow, I'll risk it. What you have to do is to get Manuela away."

"Yessir," said Gil in his best English, and admitted the surgeon with a bow. Then he went lightfooted out of the room and shut the door after him.

He was away two hours or more, and when he returned seemed perfectly happy.

"Manuela quite safa now," he told his master.

"Where is she, Gil?" he was asked, and waved his hand airily for reply.

"She all right, sir. Near 'ere. Quita safe. Presently I see 'er." He could not be brought nearer than that. Questioned on other matters, he reported that he had failed to find either Don Luis or Tormillo, and was quite unable to say how they knew of his master's relations with the Valencian girl, or what their further intentions were. His chagrin at having been found wanting in any single task set him was a great delight to Manvers and amused the slow hours of his convalescence.

His wound, which was deep but not dangerous, healed well and quickly. In ten days he was up again and inquiring for Manuela's whereabouts. Better not see her, he was advised, until it was perfectly certain that Don Luis was appeased. Gil promised that in a few days' time he would give an account of everything.

It is doubtful, however, whether he would have kept his word, had not events been too many for him. One day after dinner he asked his master if he might speak to him. On receiving permission, he drew him apart into a little room, the door of which he locked.

"Hulloa, Gil Perez," said Manvers, "what is your game now?"

"Sir," said Gil, holding his head up, and looking him full in the face. "I must espeak to you about Manuela. She is in the Carcel de la Corte—to-morrow they take 'er to the Audiencia about that assassination." He folded his arms and waited, watching the effect of his words.

Manvers was greatly perturbed. "Then you've made a mess of it," he said angrily. "You've made a mess of it."

"No mess," said Gil Perez. "She tell me must go to gaol. I say, all righta, lady."

"You had no business to say anything of the sort," Manvers said. "I am sorry I ever allowed you to interfere. I am very much annoyed with you, Perez." He had never called him Perez before—and that hurt Gil more than anything. His voice betrayed his feelings.

"You casta me off—call me Perez, lika stranger! All right, sir—what you like," he stammered. "I tell you, Manuela very fine girl—and why the devil I make 'er bad? No, sir, that imposs'. She too good for me. She say, Don Luis estab my saviour! Never, never, for me! I show Don Luis what's whata, she say. I give myself up to justice; then 'e keepa quiet—say, That's all right. So she say to Paquita—that big girl who sleep with 'er when—when——" he was embarrassed. "Mostly always sleep with 'er," he explained—"She say, 'Give me your veil, Paquita de mi alma.' Then she cover 'erself and say to me, 'Come, Gil Perez.' I say, 'Señorita, where you will.' We go to the Carcel de la Corte. Three or four alguazils in the court see 'er come in; saluta 'er, 'Good-day, señora—at the feet of your grace,' they say; for they think 'ere come a dam fine woman to see 'er lover.' She eshiver and lift 'erself. 'I am no señora,' she essay. 'Bad girl. Nama Manuela. I estab Don Bartolomé Ramonez de Alavia in the wood of La Huerca. You taka me—do what you like.' Sir, I say, thata very fine thing. I would kissa the 'and of any girl who do that—same I kiss your 'and." His voice broke. "By God, I would!"

"What next?" said Manvers, moved himself.

"Sir," said Gil Perez, "those alguazils clacka the tongue. 'Soho, la Manola!' say one, and lift 'er veil and look at 'er. All those others come and look too. They say she dam pretty woman. She standa there and look at them, lika they were dirt down in the street. Then I essay, 'Señores, you pleasa conduct this lady to the carcelero in two minutes, or you pay me, Gil Perez, 'er esservant. Thisa lady 'ave friends,' I say. 'Better for you, señores, you fetcha carcelero.' They look at me sharp—and they thinka so too. Then the carcelero 'e come, and I espeak with him and say, 'We 'ave too much money. Do what you like.'"

"And what did he do?" Manvers asked.

"He essay, 'Lady, come with me.' So then we go away witha carcelero, and I eshow my fingers—so—to those alguazils and say, 'Dam your eyes, you fellows, vayan ustedes con Dios!' Then the carcelero maka bow. 'E say to Manuela, 'Señora, you 'ave my littla room. All by yourself. My wifa she maka bed—you first-class in there. Nothing to do with them dogs down there. I give them what-for lika shot,' say the carcelero. So I pay 'im well with your bills, sir, and see Manuela all the time every day."

He took rapid strides across the room—but stopped abruptly and looked at Manvers. There was fire in his eyes. "She lika saint, sir. I catch 'er on 'er knees before our Lady of Atocha. I 'ear 'er words all broken to bits. I see 'er estrike 'er breasts—Oh, God, that make me mad! She say, 'Oh, Lady, you with your sorrow and your love—you know me very well. Bad girl, too unfortunate, too miserable—your daughter all the sama, and your lover. Give me a great 'eart, Lady, that I may tell all the truth—all—all—all! If 'e thoughta well of me,' she say, crying like one o'clock, 'let 'im know me better. No good 'e think me fine woman—no good he kissa me'"—the delicacy with which Gil Perez treated this part of the history, which Manvers had never told him, was a beautiful thing—"'I wanta tell 'im all my 'istory. Then he say, Pah, what a beast! and serva me right.' Sir, then she bow righta down to the grounda, she did, and covered 'er 'ead. I say, 'Manuela, I love you with alla my soul—but you do well, my 'eart.' And then she turn on me and tell me to go quick."

"So you are in love with her, Gil?" Manvers asked him. Gil admitted it.

"I love 'er the minute I see 'er at the *corrida*. My 'earta go alla water—but I know 'er. I say to myself, "That is la Manuela of my master Don Osmondo. You be careful, Gil Perez.'"

Manvers said, "Look here, Gil, I'm ashamed of myself. I kissed her, you know."

"Yessir," said Gil, and touched his forehead like a groom.

"If I had known that you—but I had no idea of it until this moment. I can only say——"

"Master," said Gil, "saya nothing at all. I love Manuela lika mad—that quite true; but she thinka me dirt on the pavement."

"Then she's very wrong," Manvers said.

"No, sir," said Gil, "thata true. All beautiful girls lika that. I understanda too much. But look 'ere—if she belong to me, that all the same, because I belong to you. You do what you like with 'er. I say, That all the same to me!"

"Gil Perez," said Manvers, "you're a gentleman, and I'm very much ashamed of myself. But we must do what we can for Manuela. I shall give evidence, of course. I think I can make the judge understand."

Gil was inordinately grateful, but could not conceal his nervousness. "I think the Juez, 'e too much friend with Don Luis. I think 'e know what to do all the time before. Manuela have too mucha trouble. Alla same she ver' fine girl, most beautiful, most unhappy. That do 'er good if she cry."

"I don't think she'll cry," Manvers said, and Gil Perez snorted.

"She cry! By God she never! She Espanish girl, too mucha proud, too mucha dicksure what she do with Don Bartolomé. She know she serve 'im right. Do againa all the time. What do you think 'e do with 'er when 'e 'ave 'er out there in Pobledo an' all those places? Vaya! I tell you, sir. 'E want to live on 'er. 'E wanta make 'er too bad. Then she run lika devil. Sir, I tell you what she say to me other days. 'When I saw 'im come longside Don Osmundo,' she say, 'I look in 'is face an' I see Death. 'E grin at me—then I know why 'e come. 'E talk very nice—soft, lika gentleman—then I know what 'e want. I say, Son of a dog, never!'"

"Poor girl," said Manvers, greatly concerned.

"Thata quite true, sir," Gil Perez agreed. "Very unfortunate fine girl. But you know what we say in Espain. Make yourself 'oney, we say, and the flies willa suck you. Manuela too much 'oney all the time. I know that, because she tell me everything, to tell you."

"Don't tell me," said Manvers.

"Bedam if I do," said Gil Perez.

# CHAPTER XIV

## TRIAL BY QUESTION

The court was not full when Manvers and his advocate, with Gil Perez in attendance, took their places; but it filled up gradually, and the Judge of First Instance, when he took his seat upon the tribunal, faced a throng not unworthy of a bull-fight. Bestial, leering, inflamed faces, peering eyes agog for mischief, all the nervous expectation of the sudden, the bloody or terrible were there.

There was the same dead hush when Manuela was brought in as when they throw open the doors of the *toril*, and the throng holds its breath. Gil Perez drew his with a long whistling sound, and Manvers, who could dare to look at her, thought he had never seen maidenly dignity more beautifully shown. She moved to her place with a gentle consciousness of what was due to herself very touching to see.

The crowded court thrilled and murmured, but she did not raise her eyes; once only did she show her feeling, and that was when she passed near the barrier where the spectators could have touched her by leaning over. More than one stretched his hand out, one at least his walking cane. Then she took hold of her skirt and held it back, just as a girl does when she passes wet paint. This little touch, which made the young men jeer and whisper obscenity, brought the water to Manvers' eyes. He heard Gil Perez draw again his whistling breath, and felt him tremble. Directly Manuela was in her place, standing, facing the assize, Gil Perez looked at her, and never took his eyes from her again. She was dressed in black, and her hair was smooth over her ears, knotted neatly on the nape of her neck.

The Judge, a fatigued, monumental person with a long face, pointed whiskers, and the eyes of a dead fish, told her to stand up. As she was already standing, she looked at him with patient inquiry; but he took no notice of that. Her self-possession was indeed remarkable. She gave her answers quietly, without hesitation, and when anything was asked her which offended her, either ignored it or told the questioner what she thought of it. From the outset Manvers could see that the Judge's business was to incriminate her beyond repair. Her plea of guilty was not to help her. She was to be shown infamous.

The examination ran thus:—

*Judge*: "You are Manuela, daughter of Incarnacion Presa of Valencia, and have never known your father?" (*Manuela bows her head.*) "Answer the Court."

*Manuela*: "It is true."

*Judge*: "It is said that your father was the *gitano* Sagruel?"

*Manuela*: "I don't know."

*Judge*: "You may well say that. Remember that you are condemning your mother by such answers. Your mother sold you at twelve years old to an unfrocked priest named Tormes?"

*Manuela*: "Yes. For three *pesos*."

*Judge*: "Disgraceful transaction! This wretch taught you dancing, posturing, and all manner of wickedness?"

*Manuela*: "He taught me to dance."

*Judge*: "How long were you in his company?"

*Manuela*: "For three years."

*Judge*: "He took you from fair to fair. You were a public dancer?"

*Manuela*: "That is true."

*Judge*: "I can imagine—the court can imagine—your course of life during this time. This master of yours, this Tormes, how did he treat you?"

*Manuela*: "Very ill."

*Judge*: "Be more explicit, Manuela. In what way?"

*Manuela*: "He beat me. He hurt me."

*Judge*: "Why so?"

*Manuela*: "I cannot tell you any more about him."

*Judge*: "You refuse?"

*Manuela*: "Yes."

Judge: "The court places its interpretation upon your silence." (He looked painfully round as if he regretted the absence of the proper means of extracting answers. Manvers heard Gil Perez curse him under his breath.)

The Judge made lengthy notes upon the margin of his docquet, and then proceeded.

*Judge*: "The young gentleman, Don Bartolomé Ramonez, first saw you at the fair of Salamanca in 1859?"

*Manuela*: "Yes."

*Judge*: "He saw you often, and followed you to Valladolid, where his father Don Luis lived?"

*Manuela*: "Yes."

*Judge*: "He professed his passion for you, gave you presents?"

*Manuela*: "Yes."

*Judge*: "You persuaded him to take you away from Tormes?"

*Manuela*: "No."

*Judge*: "What do I hear?"

*Manuela*: "I said 'No.' It was because he said that he loved me that I went with him. He wished to marry me, he said."

*Judge*: "What! Don Bartolomé Ramonez marry a public dancer! Be careful what you say there, Manuela."

*Manuela*: "He told me so, and I believed him."

*Judge*: "I pass on. You were with him until the April of this year—you were with him two years?"

*Manuela*: "Yes."

*Judge*: "And then you found another lover and deserted him?"

*Manuela*: "No. I ran away from him by myself."

*Judge*: "But you found another lover?"

*Manuela*: "No."

*Judge*: "Be careful, Manuela. You will trip in a moment. You ran away from Don Bartolomé when you were at Pobledo, and you went to Palencia. What did you do there?"

*Manuela*: "I cannot answer you."

*Judge*: "You mean that you will not?"

*Manuela*: "I mean that I cannot."

*Judge*: "This is wilful prevarication again. I have authority to compel you."

*Manuela*: "You have none."

*Judge*: "We shall see, Manuela, we shall see. You left Palencia on the 12th of May in the company of an Englishman?"

*Manuela*: "Yes."

*Judge*: "He is here in court?"

*Manuela*: "Yes."

*Judge*: "Do you see him at this moment?"

*Manuela*: "Yes." (But she did not turn her head to look at Manvers until the Judge forced her.)

*Judge*: "I am not he. I am not likely to have taken you from Palencia and your proceedings there. Look at the Englishman." (She hesitated for a little while, and then turned her eyes upon him with such gentle modesty that Manvers felt nearer to loving her than he had ever done. He rose slightly in his seat and bowed to her: she returned the salute like a young queen. The Judge had gained nothing by that.) "I see that you treat each other with ceremony; there may be reasons for that. We shall soon see. This gentleman then took you away from Palencia in the direction of Valladolid, and made you certain proposals. What were they?"

*Manuela*: "He proposed that I should return to Palencia."

*Judge*: "And you refused?"

*Manuela*: "Yes."

*Judge*: "Why?"

*Manuela*: "I could not go back to Palencia."

*Judge*: "Why?"

*Manuela*: "There were many reasons. One was that I was afraid of seeing Estéban there."

*Judge*: "You mean Don Bartolomé Ramonez de, Alavia?" (She nodded.) "Answer me."

*Manuela*: "Yes, yes."

*Judge*: "You are impatient because your evil deeds are coming to light. I am not surprised; but you must command yourself. There is more to come." (Manvers, who was furious, asked his advocate whether something could not be done. Directly her fear of Estéban was touched upon, he said, the Judge changed his tactics. The advocate smiled. "Be patient, sir," he said. "The Judge has been instructed beforehand." "You mean," said

Manvers, "that he has been bribed?" "I did not say so," the advocate replied.)

The Judge returned to Palencia. "What other reasons had you?" was his next question, but Manuela was clever enough to see where her strength lay. "My fear of Estéban swallowed all other reasons." She saved herself, and with unconcealed chagrin the Judge went on towards the real point.

*Judge*: "The Englishman then made you another proposal?"

*Manuela*: "Yes, sir. He proposed to take me to a convent."

*Judge*: "You refused that?"

*Manuela*: "No, sir. I should have been glad to go to a convent."

*Judge*: "You, however, accepted his third proposal, namely, that you should be under his protection?"

*Manuela*: "I was thankful for his protection when I saw Estéban coming."

*Judge*: "I have no doubt of that. You had reason to fear Don Bartolomé's resentment?"

*Manuela*: "I knew that Estéban intended to murder me."

*Judge*: "Don Bartolomé overtook you. You were riding before the Englishman on his horse?"

*Manuela*: "Yes. I could not walk. I was ill."

*Judge*: "Don Bartolomé remained with you until the Englishman ran away?"

*Manuela*: "He did not run away. Why should he? He went away on his own affairs."

*Judge* (after looking at his papers): "I see. The Englishman went away after the pair of you had killed Don Bartolomé?"

*Manuela*: "That is not true. He went away to bathe, and then I killed Estéban with his own knife. I killed him because he told me that he intended to murder me, and the English gentleman who had been kind to me. I confess it—I confessed it to the *alguazils* and the *carcelero*. You may twist what I say as you will, to please your friends, but the truth is in what I say."

*Judge*: "Silence! It is for you to answer the questions which I put to you. You forget yourself, Manuela. But I will take your confession as true for the moment. Supposing it to be true, did you not stab Don Bartolomé in the neck in order that you might be free?"

*Manuela*: "I killed him to defend myself and an innocent person. I have told you so."

*Judge*: "Why should Don Bartolomé wish to kill you?"

*Manuela*: "He hated me because I had refused to do his pleasure. He wished to make me bad——"

*Judge* (lifting his hands and throwing his head up): "Bad! Was he not jealous of the Englishman?"

*Manuela*: "I don't know."

*Judge*: "Did he not tell you that the Englishman was your lover? Did you not say so to Fray Juan de la Cruz?"

*Manuela*: "He spoke falsely. It was not true. He may have believed it."

*Judge*: "We shall see. Have patience, Manuela. Having slain your old lover, you were careful to leave a token for his successor. You left more than that: your crucifix from your neck, and a message with Fray Juan?"

*Manuela*: "Yes. I told Fray Juan the whole of the truth, and begged him to tell the gentleman, because I wished him to think well of me. I told him that Estéban——"

*Judge*: "Softly, softly, Manuela. Why did you leave your crucifix behind you?"

*Manuela*: "Because I was grateful to the gentleman who had saved my life at Palencia; because I had nothing else to give him. Had I had anything more valuable I would have left it. Nobody had been kind to me before."

*Judge*: "You know what he has done with your crucifix, Manuela?"

*Manuela*: "I do not."

*Judge*: "What are you saying?"

*Manuela*: "The truth."

*Judge*: "I have the means of confuting you. You told Fray Juan that you were going to Madrid?"

*Manuela*: "I did not."

*Judge*: "In the hope that he would tell the Englishman?"

*Manuela*: "If he told the gentleman that, he lied."

*Judge*: "It is then a singular coincidence which led to your meeting him here in Madrid?"

*Manuela*: "I did not meet him."

*Judge*: "Did you not meet him a few nights before you surrendered to justice?"

*Manuela*: "No."

*Judge*: "Did you meet his servant?"

*Manuela*: "I cannot tell you."

*Judge*: "Did not the Englishman pay for your lodging in the Carcel de la Corte? Did he not send his servant every day to see you?"

*Manuela*: "The gentleman was lying wounded at the hotel. He had been stabbed in the street."

*Judge*: "We are not discussing the Englishman's private affairs. Answer my questions?"

*Manuela*: "I cannot answer them."

*Judge*: "You mean that you will not, Manuela. Did you not know that the Englishman caused your crucifix to be set in gold, like a holy relic?"

*Manuela*: "I did not know it."

*Judge*: "We have it on your own confession that you slew Don Bartolomé Ramonez in the wood of La Huerca, and you admit that the Englishman was protecting you before that dreadful deed was done, that he has since paid for your treatment in prison, and that he has treasured your crucifix like a sacred relic?"

*Manuela*: "You are pleased to say these things. I don't say them. You wish to incriminate a person who has been kind to me."

*Judge*: "I will ask you one more question, Manuela. Why did you give yourself up to justice?"

*Manuela* (after a painful pause, speaking with high fervour and some approach to dramatic effect): "I will answer you, señor Juez. It was because I knew that Don Luis would contrive the death of Don Osmundo if I did not prove him innocent."

*Judge* (rising, very angry): "Silence! The court cannot entertain your views of persons not concerned in your crime."

*Manuela*: "But——" (She shrugged, and looked away.)

*Judge*: "You can sit down."

# CHAPTER XV

## NEMESIS—DON LUIS

Manvers' reiterated question of how in the name of wonder Don Luis or anybody else knew what he had done with Manuela's crucifix was answered before the day was over; but not by Gil Perez or the advocate whom he had engaged to defend the unhappy girl.

This personage gave him to understand without disguise that there was very little chance for Manuela. The Judge, he said, had been "instructed." He clung to that phrase. When Manvers said, "Let us instruct him a little," he took snuff and replied that he feared previous "instruction" might have created a prejudice. He undertook, however, to see him privately before judgment was delivered, but intimated that he must have a very free hand.

Manvers' rejoinder took the shape of a blank cheque with his signature upon it. The advocate, fanning himself with it in an abstracted manner, went on to advise the greatest candour in the witness-box. "Beware of irritation, dear sir," he said. "The Judge will plant a banderilla here and there, you may be sure. That is his method. You learn more from an angry man than a cool one. For my own part," he went on, "you know how we stand—without witnesses. I shall do what I can, you may be sure."

"I hope you will get something useful from the prisoner," Manvers said. "A little of Master Estéban's private history should be useful."

"It would be perfectly useless, if you will allow me to say so," replied the advocate. "The Judge will not hear a word against a family like the Ramonez. So noble and so poor! Perhaps you are not aware that the Archbishop of Toledo is Don Luis' first cousin? That is so."

"But is that allowed to justify his rip of a son in goading a girl on to murder?" cried Manvers.

The advocate again took snuff, shrugging as he tapped his fingers on the box. "The Ramonez say, you see, sir, that Don Bartolomé may have threatened her, moved by jealousy. Jealousy is a well-understood passion here. The plea is valid and good."

"Might it not stand for Manuela too?" he was asked.

"I don't think we had better advance it, Don Osmundo," he said, after a significant pause.

Gil Perez, pale and all on edge, had been walking the room like a caged wolf. He swore to himself—but in English, out of politeness to his master. "Thata dam thief! Ah, Juez of my soul, if I see you twist in 'ell is good for me." Presently he took Manvers aside and, his eyes full of tears, asked him, "Sir, you escusa Manuela, if you please. She maka story ver' bad to 'ear. She no like—I see 'er red as fire, burn like the devil, sir. She ver' unfortunata girl—too beautiful to live. And all these 'ogs—Oh, my God, what can she do?" He opened his arms, and turned his pinched face to the sky. "What can she do, Oh, my God?" he cried. "So beautiful as a rose, an' so poor, and so a child! You sorry, sir, hey?" he asked, and Manvers said he was more sorry than he could say.

That comforted him. He kissed his master's hand, and then told him that Manuela was glad that he knew all about her. "She dam glad, sir, that I know. She say to me las' night—'What I shall tell the Juez will be the very truth. Señor Don Osmundo shall know what I am,' she say. 'To 'im I could never say it. To thata Juez too easy say it. To-morrow,' she say, "e know me for what I am—too bad girl!'"

"I think she is a noble girl," said Manvers. "She's got more courage in her little finger than I have in my body. She's a girl in a thousand."

Gil Perez glowed, and lifted up his beaten head. "Esplendid—eh?" he cried out. "By God, I serve 'er on my knees!"

On returning to the court, the beard and patient face of Fray Juan greeted our friend. He had very little to testify, save that he was sure the Englishman had known nothing of the crime. The prisoner had told him her story without haste or passion. He had been struck by that. She said that she killed. Don Bartolomé in a hurry lest he should kill both her and her benefactor. She had not informed him, nor had he reported to the gentleman, that she was going to Madrid. The Englishman said that he intended to find her, and witness had strongly advised him against it. He had told him that his motives would be misunderstood. "As, in fact, they have been, brother?" the advocate suggested. Fray Juan raised his eyebrows, and sighed. "*Quien sabe?*" was his answer.

Manvers then stood up and spoke his testimony. He gave the facts as the reader knows then, and made it clear that Manuela was in terror of Estéban from the moment he appeared, and even before he appeared. He had noticed that she frequently glanced behind them as they rode, and had asked her the reason. Her fear of him in the wood was manifest, and he blamed himself greatly for leaving her alone with the young man.

"I was new to the country, you must understand," he said. "I could see that there was some previous acquaintance between those two, but could not guess that it was so serious. I thought, however, that they had made up their differences and gone off together when I returned from bathing. When Pray Juan showed me the body and told me what had been done I was very much shocked. It had been, in one sense, my fault, for if I had not rescued her, Estéban would not have suspected me, or intended my death. That I saw at once; and my desire of meeting Manuela again was that I might defend her from the consequences of an act which I had, in that one sense, brought about—to which she had, at any rate, been driven on my account."

"I will ask you, sir," said the Judge, "one question upon that. Was that also your motive in having the crucifix set in pure gold?"

"No," said Manvers, "not altogether. I doubt if I can explain that to you."

"I am of that opinion myself," said the Judge, with an elaborate bow. "But the court will be interested to hear you."

The court was.

"This girl," Manvers said, "was plainly most unfortunate. She was ragged, poorly fed, had been ill-used, and was being shamefully handled when I first saw her. I snatched her out of the hands of the wretches who would have torn her to pieces if I had not interfered. From beginning to end I never saw more shocking treatment of a woman than I saw at Palencia. Not to have interfered would have shamed me for life. What then? I rescued her, as I say, and she showed herself grateful in a variety of ways. Then Estéban Vincaz came up and chose to treat me as her lover. I believe he knew better, and think that my horse and haversack had more to do with it. Well, I left Manuela with him in the wood—hardly, I may suggest, the act of a lover—and never saw Estéban alive again. But I believe Manuela's story absolutely; I am certain she would not lie at such a time, or to such a man as Fray Juan. The facts were extraordinary, and her crime, done as it was in defence of myself, was heroic—or I thought so. Her leaving of the crucifix was, to me, a proof of her honest intention. I valued the gift, partly for the sake of the giver, partly for the act which it commemorated. She had received a small service from me, and had returned it fifty-fold by an act of desperate courage. To crown her charity, she left me all that she had in the world. I do not wonder myself at what I did. I took the crucifix to a jeweller at Valladolid, had it set as I thought it deserved—and I see now that I did her there a cruel wrong."

"Permit me to say, sir," said the triumphant Judge, "that you also did Don Luis Ramonez a great service. Through your act, however intended, he has been enabled to bring a criminal to justice."

"I beg pardon," said Manvers, "she brought herself to justice—so soon as Don Luis Ramonez sent his assassin out to stab me in the back, and in the dark. And this again was a proof of her heroism, since she thought by these means to satisfy his craving for human blood."

Manvers spoke incisively and with severity. The court thrilled, and the murmuring was on his side. The Judge was much disturbed. Manuela alone maintained her calm, sitting like a pensive Hebe, her cheek upon her hand.

The Judge's annoyance was extreme. It tempted him to wrangle.

"I beg you, sir, to restrain yourself. The court cannot listen to extraneous matter. It is concerned with the consideration of a serious crime. The illustrious gentleman of your reference mourns the loss of his only son."

"I fail," said Manvers, "to see how my violent death can assuage his grief." The Judge was not the only person in court to raise his eyebrows; if Manvers had not been angry he would have seen the whole assembly in the same act, and been certified that they were not with him now. His advocate whispered him urgently to sit down. He did, still mystified. The Judge immediately retired to consider his judgment.

Manvers' advocate left the court and was away for an hour. He returned very sedately to his place, with the plainly expressed intention of saying nothing. The court buzzed with talk, much of it directed at the beautiful prisoner, whose person, bearing, motives, and fate were freely discussed. Oddly enough, at that moment, half the men in the hall were ready to protect her.

Manvers felt his heart beating, but could neither think nor speak coherently. If Manuela were to be condemned to death, what was he to do? He knew not at all; but the crisis to which his own affairs and his own life were now brought turned him cold. He dared not look at Gil Perez. The minutes dragged on——

The Judge entered the court and sat in his chair. He looked very much like a codfish—with his gaping mouth and foolish eyes. He pulled one of his long whiskers and inspected the end of it; detected a split hair, separated it from its happier fellows, shut his eyes, gave a vicious wrench to it and gasped as it parted. Then he stared at the assembly before him, as if to catch them laughing, frowned at Manvers, who sat before him with folded arms; lastly he turned to the prisoner, who stood up and looked him in the face.

"Manuela," he said, "you stand condemned upon your own confession of murder in the first degree—murder of a gentleman who had been your benefactor, of whose life and protection you desired, for reasons of your own, to be ridded. The court is clear that you are guilty and cannot give you any assurance that your surrender to justice has assisted the ministers of justice. Those diligent guardians would have found you sooner or later, you may be sure. If anyone is to be thanked it is, perhaps, the foreign gentleman, whose candour"—and here he had the assurance to make Manvers a bow—"whose candour, I say, has favourably impressed the court. But, nevertheless, the court, in its clemency, is willing to allow you the merits of your intention. It is true that justice would have been done without your confession; but it may be allowed that you desired to stand well with the laws, after having violated them in an outrageous manner. It is this desire of yours which inclines the court to mercy. I shall not inflict the last penalty upon you, nor exact the uttermost farthing which your crime deserves. The court is willing to believe that you are penitent, and condemns you to perpetual seclusion in the Institution of the Recogidas de Santa Maria Magdalena."

Manuela was seen to close her eyes; but she collected herself directly. She looked once, piercingly, at Manvers, then surrendered herself to him who touched her on the shoulder, turned, and went out of the court.

Everybody was against her now: they jeered, howled, hissed and cursed her. A spoiled plaything had got its deserts. Manvers turned upon them in a white fury. "Dogs," he cried, "will nothing shame you?" But nobody seemed to hear or heed him at the moment, and Gil Perez whispered in his ear, "That no good, master. This *canalla* all the same swine. You come with me, sir, I tell you dam good thing." He had recovered his old jauntiness, and swaggered before his master, clearing the way with oaths and threatenings.

Manvers followed him in a very stern mood. By the door he felt a touch on the arm, and turning, saw a tall, elderly gentleman cloaked in black. He recognised him at once by his hollow eye-sockets and smouldering, deeply set eyes. "You will remember me, señor caballero, in the shop of Sebastian the goldsmith," he said; and Manvers admitted it. He received another bow, and the reminder. "We met again, I think, in the Church of Las Angustias in Valladolid."

"Yes, indeed," Manvers said, "I remember you very well."

"Then you remember, no doubt, saying to me with regard to your crucifix, which I had seen in Sebastian's hands, then in your own, that it was a piece of extravagance on your part. You will not withdraw that statement to-day, I suppose."

That which lay latent in his words was betrayed by the gleam of cold fire in his eyes. Manvers coloured. "You have this advantage of me, señor," he said, "that you know to whom you are speaking, and I do not."

"It is very true, señor Don Osmundo," the gentleman said severely. "I will enlighten you. I am Don Luis Ramonez de Alavia, at your service."

Manvers turned white. He had indeed made Manuela pay double. So much for sentiment in Spain.

# CHAPTER XVI

## THE HERALD

A card of ample size and flourished characters, bearing the name of El Marqués de Fuenterrabia, was brought up by Gil Perez.

"Who is he?" Manvers inquired; and Gil waved his hand.

"This olda gentleman," he explained, "'e come Embassador from Don Luis. 'E say, 'What you do next, señor Don Osmundo?' You tell 'im, sir—is my advice."

"But I don't know what I am going to do," said Manvers irritably. "How the deuce should I know?"

"You tell 'im that, sir," Gil said softly. "Thata best of all."

"What do you mean?"

"I mean, sir, then 'e tell you what Don Luis, 'e do."

"Show him in," said Manvers.

The Marqués de Fuenterrabia was a white-whiskered, irascible personage, of stately manners and slight stature. He wore a blue frock-coat, and nankeen trousers over riding-boots. His face was one uniform pink, his eyes small, fierce, and blue. They appeared to emit heat as well as light; for it was a frequent trick of their proprietor's to snatch at his spectacles and wipe the mist from them with a bandana handkerchief. Unglazed, his eyes showed a blank and indiscriminate ferocity which Manvers found exceedingly comical.

They bowed to each other—the Marqués with ceremonious cordiality, Manvers with the stiffness of an Englishman to an unknown visitor. Gil Perez hovered in the background, as it were, on the tips of his toes.

The Marqués, having made his bow, said nothing. His whole attitude seemed to imply, "Well, what next?"

Manvers said that he was at his service; and then the Marqués explained himself.

"My friend, Don Luis Ramonez de Alavia," he said, "has entrusted me with his confidence. It appears that a series of occurrences, involving his happiness, honour and dignity at once, can be traced to your

Excellency's intromission in his affairs. I take it that your Excellency does not deny——"

"Pardon me," Manvers said, "I deny it absolutely."

The Marqués was very much annoyed. "*Que! Que!*" he muttered and snatched off his spectacles. Glaring ferociously at them, he wiped them with his bandana.

"If Don Luis really imagines that I compassed the death of his son," said Manvers, "I suppose he has his legal remedy. He had better have me arrested and have done with it."

The Marqués, his spectacles on, gazed at the speaker with astonishment. "Is it possible, sir, that you can so misconceive the mind of a gentleman as to suggest legal process in an affair of the kind? Whatever my friend Don Luis may consider you, he could not be guilty of such a discourtesy. One may think he is going too far in the other direction, indeed—though one is debarred from saying so under the circumstances. But I am not here to bandy words with you. My friend Don Luis commissions me to ask your Excellency, for the name of a friend, to whom the arrangements may be referred for ending a painful controversy in the usual manner. If you will be so good as to oblige me, I need not intrude upon you again."

"Do you mean to suggest, señor Marqués," said Manvers, after a pause, "that I am to meet Don Luis on the field?"

"Pardon?" said the Marqués, in such a way as to answer the question.

"My dear sir," he was assured, "I would just as soon fight my grandfather. The thing is preposterous." The Marqués gasped for air, but Manvers continued. "Had your friend's age been anywhere near my own, I doubt if I could have gratified him after what took place the other day. He caused a man of his to stab me in the back as I was walking down a dark street. In my country we call that a dastard's act."

The Marqués started, and winced as if he was hurt; but he remembered himself and the laws of warfare, and when he spoke it was within the extremes of politeness.

"I confess, sir," he said, "that I was not prepared for your refusal. It puts me in a delicate position, and to a certain extent I must involve my friend also. It is my duty to declare to you that it is Don Luis' intention to break the laws of Spain. An outrage has been committed against his house and blood which one thing only can efface. Moved by extreme courtesy, Don Luis was prepared to take the remedy of gentlemen; but since you have refused him that, he is driven to the use of natural law. It will be in your power—I cannot deny—to deprive him of that also; but he is persuaded that you will not take advantage of it. Should you show any signs of doing so, I am to say, Don Luis will be forced to consider you outside the pale of civilisation, and to treat you without any kind of toleration. To suggest such a possibility is painful to me, and I beg your pardon very truly for it."

In truth the Marqués looked ashamed of himself.

Manvers considered the very oblique oration to which he had listened. "I hope I understand you, señor Marqués," he said. "You intend to say that Don Luis means to have my life by all means?"

The Marqués bowed. "That is so, señor Don Osmundo."

"But you suggest that it is possible that I might stop him by informing the authorities?"

"No, no," said the Marqués hastily, "I did not suggest that. The authorities would never interfere. The British Embassy might perhaps be persuaded—but you will do me the justice to admit that I apologised for the suggestion."

"Oh, by all means," said Manvers. "You thought pretty badly of me—but not so badly as all that."

"Quite so," said the Marqués; and then the surprising Gil Perez descended from mid-air, and lowed to the stranger.

"My master, Don Osmundo, señor Marqués, is incapable of such conduct," said he—and looked to Manvers for approval.

He struggled with himself, but failed. His guffaw must out, and exploded with violent effect. It drove the Marqués back to the door, and sent Gil Perez scudding on tiptoe to the window.

"You are magnificent, all of you!" cried Manvers. "You flatter me into connivance. Let me state the case exactly. Don Luis is to stab or shoot me at sight, and I am to give him a free hand. Is that what you mean? Admirable. But let me ask you one question. Am I not supposed to protect myself?"

The Marqués stared. "I don't think I perfectly understand you, Don Osmundo. Reprisals are naturally open to you. We declare war, that is all."

"Oh," said Manvers. "You declare war? Then I may go shooting, too?"

"Naturally," said the Marqués. "That is understood."

"No dam fear about that," said Gil Perez to his master.

# CHAPTER XVII

## LA RECOGIDA

Sister Chucha, the nun who took first charge of newcomers to the Penitentiary, was fat and kindly, and not very discreet. It was her business to measure Manuela for a garb and to see to the cutting of her hair. She told the girl that she was by far the most handsome penitent she had ever had under her hands.

"It is a thousand pities to cut all this beauty away," she said; "for it is obvious you will want it before long. So far as that goes you will find the cap not unbecoming; and I'll see to it that you have a piece of looking-glass—though, by ordinary, that is forbidden. Good gracious, child, what a figure you have! If I had had one quarter of your good fortune I should never have been religious."

She went on to describe the rules of the Institution, the hours and nature of the work, the offices in Chapel, the recreation times and hours for meals. Manuela, she said, was not the build for rope and mat work.

"I shall get Reverend Mother to put you to housework, I think," she said. "That will give you exercise, and the chance of an occasional peep at the window. You don't deserve it, I fancy; but you are so handsome that I have a weakness for you. All you have to do is to speak fairly to Father Vicente and curtsey to the Reverend Mother whenever you see her. Above all, no tantrums. Leave the others alone, and they'll let you alone. There's not one of them but has her scheme for getting away, or her friend outside. That's occupation enough for her. It will be the same with you. Your friends will find you out. You'll have a *novio* spending the night in the street before to-morrow's over unless I am very much mistaken." She patted her cheek. "I'll do what I can for you, my dear."

Manuela curtseyed, and thanked the good nun. "All I have to do," she said, "is to repent of my sin—which has become very horrible to me."

"La-la-la!" cried Sister Chucha. "Keep that for Father Vicente, if you please, my dear. That is his affair. Our patroness led a jolly life before she was a saint. No doubt, you should not have stabbed Don Bartolomé, and of course the Ramonez would never overlook such a thing. But we all understand that you must save your own skin if you could—that's very reasonable. And I hear that there was another reason." Here she chucked her chin. "I don't wonder at it," she said with a meaning smile.

The girl coloured and hung her head. She was still quivering with the shame of her public torture. She could still see Manvers' eyes stare chilly at the wall before them, and believe them to grow colder with each stave of her admissions. Her one consolation lay in the thought that she could please him by amendment and save him by a conviction; so it was hard to be petted by Sister Chucha. She would have welcomed the whip, would have hugged it to her bosom—the rod of Salvation, she would have called it; but compliments on her beauty, caresses of cheek and chin—was she not to be allowed to be good? As for escape, she had no desire for that. She could love her Don Osmundo best from a distance. What was to be gained, but shame, by seeing him?

Her shining hair was cut off; the cap, the straight prison garb were put on. She stood up, slim-necked, an arrowy maid, with her burning face and sea-green eyes chastened by real humility. She made a good confession to Father Vicente, and took her place among her mates.

It was true, what Sister Chucha had told her. Every penitent in that great and gaunt building was thrilled with one persistent hope, worked patiently with that in view, and under its spell refrained from violence or clamour. There was not one face of those files of grey-gowned girls which, at stated hours, entered the chapel, knelt at the altar, or stooped at painful labour through the stifling days, which did not show a gleam. Stupid, vacant, vicious, morose, pretty, sparkling, whatever the face might be, there was that expectation to redeem or enhance it, to make it human, to make it womanish. There was, or there would be, some day, any day, a lover outside—to whom it would be the face of all faces.

Manuela had not been two hours in the company of her fellow-prisoners before she was told that there were two ways of escape from the Recogidas. Religion or marriage these were; but the religious alternative was not discussed.

Sister Chucha, it transpired, had chosen that way—"But do you wonder?" cried the girl who told Manuela, with shrill scorn. Most of the sisters had once been penitents—"*Vaya!* Look at them, my dear!" cried this young Amazon, conscious of her own charms.

She was a plump Andalusian, black-eyed, merry, and quick to change her moods. Love had sent her to Saint Mary Magdalene, and love would take her out again.

That Chucha, she owned, was a kind soul. She always put the pretty ones to housework—"it gives us a chance at the windows. I have Fernando, who works at the sand-carting in the river. He never fails to look up this way. Some day he will ask for me." She peered at herself in a pail of water, and fingered her cap daintily. "How does my skirt hang now, Manuela? Too short, I fancy. Did you ever see such shoes as they give you here! Lucky that nobody can see you."

This was the strain of everybody's talk in the House of Las Recogidas—in the whitewashed galleries where they walked in squads under the eye of a nun who sat reading a good book against the wall, in the court where they lay in the shade to rest, prone, with their faces hidden in their arms, or with knees huddled up and eyes fixed in a stare. They talked to each other in the hoarse, tearful staccato of Spain, which, beginning low, seems to gather force and volume as it runs, until, like a beck in flood, it carries speaker and listener over the bar and into tossing waves of yeasty water.

Manuela, through all, kept her thoughts to herself, and spoke nothing of her own affairs. There may have been others like her, fixed to the great achievement of justifying themselves to their own standard: she had no means of knowing. Her standard was this, that she had purged herself by open confession to the man whom she loved. She was clean, sweetened and full of heart. All she had to do was to open wide her house that holiness might enter in.

Besides this she had, at the moment, the consciousness of a good action; for she firmly believed that by her surrender to the law she had again saved Manvers from assassination. If Don Luis could only cleanse his honour by blood, he now had her heart's blood. That should suffice him. She grew happier as the days went on.

Meanwhile it was remarked upon by Mercédes and Dolores, and half a dozen more, that distinguished strangers came to the gallery of the chapel. The outlines of them could be descried through the *grille*; for behind the *grille* was a great white window which threw them into high relief.

It was the fixed opinion of Mercédes and Dolores that Manuela had a *novio*.

# CHAPTER XVII

## THE NOVIO

It is true that Manvers had gone to the Chapel of the Recogidas to look for, or to look at, Manuela. This formed the one amusing episode in his week's round in Madrid, where otherwise he was extremely bored, and where he only remained to give Don Luis a chance of waging his war.

To be shot at in the street, or stabbed in the back as you are homing through the dusk are, to be sure, not everybody's amusements, and in an ordinary way they were not those of Mr. Manvers. But he found that his life gained a zest by being threatened with deprivation, and so long as that zest lasted he was willing to oblige Don Luis. The weather was insufferably hot, one could only be abroad early in the morning or late at night—both the perfection of seasons for the assassin's game.

Yet nothing very serious had occurred during the week following the declaration of war. Gil Perez could not find Tormillo, and had to declare that his suspicions of a Manchegan teamster, who had jostled his master in the Puerta del Sol and made as if to draw his knife, were without foundation. What satisfied him was that the Manchegan, that same evening, stabbed somebody else to death. "That show 'e is good fellow—too much after 'is enemy," said Gil Perez affably. So Manvers felt justified in his refusal to wear mail or carry either revolver or sword-stick; and by the end of the week he forgot that he was a marked man.

On Sunday he told Gil Perez that he intended to visit the Chapel of the Recogidas.

The rogue's face twinkled. "Good, sir, good. We go. I show you Manuela all-holy like a nun. I know whata she do. Look for 'eaven all day. That Chucha she tell me something—and the *portero*, 'e damgood fellow."

Resplendent in white duck trousers, Mr. Manvers was remarked upon by a purely native company of sightseers. Quick-eyed ladies in mantillas were there, making play with their fans and scent-bottles; attendant cavaliers found something of which to whisper in the cool-faced Englishman with his fair beard, blue eyes, and eye-glass, his air of detachment, which disguised his real feelings, and of readiness to be entertained, which they misinterpreted.

The facts were that he was painfully involved in Manuela's fate, and uncomfortably near being in love again with the lovely unfortunate. She was no longer a pretty thing to be kissed, no longer even a handsome murderess; she was become a heroine, a martyr, a thing enskied and sainted.

He had seen more than he had been meant to see during his ordeal in the Audiencia—her consciousness of himself, for instance, as revealed in that last dying look she had given him, that long look before she turned and followed her gaolers out of court. He guessed at her agonies of shame, he understood how it was that she had courted it; in fine, he knew very well that her heart was in his keeping—and that's a dangerous possession for a man already none too sure of the whereabouts of his own.

When the organ music thrilled and opened, and the Recogidas filed in—some hundred of them—his heart for a moment stood still, as he scanned them through the gloom. They were dressed exactly alike in dull clinging grey, all wore close-fitting white caps, were nearly all dead-white in the face. They all shuffled, as convicts do when they move close-ordered to their work afield.

It shocked him that he utterly failed to identify Manuela—and it brought him sharply to his better senses that Gil Perez saw her at once. "See her there, master, see there my beautiful," the man groaned under his breath, and Manvers looked where he pointed, and saw her; but now the glamour was gone. Gil was her declared lover. The Squire of Somerset could not stoop to be his valet's rival.

The Squire of Somerset, however, observed that she held herself more stiffly than her co-mates, and shuffled less. The prison garb clothed her like a weed; she had the trick of wearing clothes so that they draped the figure, not concealed it, were as wax upon it, not a cerement. That which fell shapeless and heavily from the shoulders of the others, upon her seemed to grow rather from the waist—to creep upwards over the shoulders, as ivy steals clinging over a statue in a park. Here, said he, is a maiden that cannot be hid. Call her a murderess, she remains perfect woman; call her convict, Magdalen, she is some man's solace. He looked: at Gil Perez, motionless and intent by his side, and heard his short breath: There is her mate, he thought to himself, and was saved.

They filed out as they had come in. They all stood, turned towards the exit, and waited until they were directed to move. Then they followed each other like sheep through a gateway, looking, so far as he could see, at nothing, expecting nothing, and remembering nothing. A down-trodden herd, he conceived them, their wits dulled by toil. He was not near enough to see the gleam which kept them alive. Nuns gave them their orders with authoritative hands, quick always, and callous by routine, probably not intended to be so harsh as they appeared. He saw one girl pushed forward by the shoulder with such suddenness that she nearly fell; another flinched at a passionate command; another scowled as she passed her mistress. He watched to see how Manuela, who had come in one of the first and must go out one of the last, would bear herself, and was relieved by a pretty and enheartening episode.

Manuela, as she passed, drew her hand along the top of the bench with a lingering, trailing touch. It encountered that of the nun in command, and he saw the nun's hand enclose and press the penitent's. He saw Manuela's look of gratitude, and the nun's smiling affection; he believed that Manuela blushed. That gratified him extremely, and enlarged his benevolent intention.

Had Gil Perez seen it? He thought not. Gil Perez' black eyes were fixed upon Manuela's form. They glittered like a cat's when he watches a bird in a shrubbery. The valet was quite unlike himself as he followed his master homewards and asked leave of absence for the evening—for the first time in his period of service. Manvers had no doubt at all how that evening was spent—in rapt attention below the barred windows of the House of the Recogidas.

That was so. Gil Perez "played the bear," as they call it, from dusk till the small hours—perfectly happy, in a rapture of adoration which the Squire of Somerset could never have realised. All the romance which, if we may believe Cervantes, once transfigured the life of Spain, and gilded the commonest acts till they seemed confident appeals for the applause of God, feats boldly done under Heaven's thronged barriers, is nowadays concentred in this one strange vigil which all lovers have to keep.

Gil Perez the quick, the admirable servant, the jaunty adventurer, the assured rogue, had vanished. Here he stood beneath the stars, breathing prayers and praises—not a little valet sighing for a convicted Magdalen, but a young knight keeping watch beneath his lady's tower. And he was not alone there: at due intervals along the frowning walls were posted other servants of the sleeping girls behind them; other knights at watch and ward.

The prayer he breathed was the prayer breathed too for Dolores or Mercédes in prison. "Virgin of Atocha, Virgin of the Pillar, Virgin of Sorrow, of Divine Compassion, send happy sleep to thy handmaid Manuela, shed the dew of thy love upon her eyelids, keep smooth her brows, keep innocent her lips. Dignify me, thy servant, Gil Perez, more than other men, that I may be worthy to sustain this high honour of love."

His eyes never wavered from a certain upper window. It was as blank as all the rest, differed in no way from any other of a row of five-and-twenty. To him if was the pride of the great building.

"O fortunate stars!" he whispered to himself, "that can look through these and see my love upon her bed. O rays too much blessed, that can kiss her eyelids, and touch lightly upon the scented strands of her hair! O breath of the night, that can fan in her white neck and stroke her arm stretched out over the coverlet! To you, night-wind, and to you, stars, I give an errand; you shall take a message from me to lovely Manuela of the golden tresses. Tell her that I am watching out the dark; tell her that no harm shall come to her. Whisper in her ear, mingle with her dreams, and tell her that she has a lover. Tell her also that the nights in Madrid are not like those in Valencia, and that she would do well to cover her arm and shoulder up lest she catch cold, and suffer."

There spoke the realist, the romantic realist of Spain; for it is to be observed that Gil Perez did not know at all whereabouts Manuela lay asleep, and could not, naturally, know whether her arm was out of bed or in it. He had forgotten also that her hair had been cut off—but these are trifles. Happy he! he had forgotten much more than that.

When Manvers told him that he intended to pay Manuela a visit on the day allowed, Gil Perez suffered the tortures of the damned. Jealous rage consumed his vitals like a corroding acid, which reason and loyalty had no power to assuage. Yet reason and loyalty played out their allotted parts, and it had been a fine sight to see Gil grinning and gibbering at his own white face in the looking-glass, shaking his finger at it and saying to it, in English (since it was his master's shaving-glass), "Gil Perez, my fellow, you shut up!" He said it many times, for he had nothing else to say—jealousy deprived him of his wits; and he felt better for the discipline. When Manvers returned there was no sign upon Gil's brisk person of the stormy conflict which had ravaged it.

Manvers had seen her and, by Sister Chucha's charity, had seen her alone. The poor girl had fallen at his feet and would have kissed them if he had not lifted her up. "No, my dear, no," he said; "it is I who ought to kneel. You have done wonders for me. You are as brave as a lion, Manuela; but I must get you away from this place."

"No, no, Don Osmundo," she cried, flushing up, "indeed I am better here." She stood before him, commanding herself, steeling herself in the presence of this man she loved against any hint of her beating heart.

He had himself well in hand. Her beauty, her distress and misfortune could not touch him now. All that he had for her was admiration and pure benevolence. Fatal offerings for a woman inflamed: so soon as she perceived it her courage was needed for another tussle. Her blood lay like lead in her veins, her heart sank to the deeps of her, and she must screw it back again to the work of the day.

He took her hand, and she let him have it. What could it matter now what he had of hers? "Manuela," he said, "there is a way of freedom for you, if you will take it. A man loves you truly, and asks nothing better than to work for you. I know him; he's been a good friend to me. Will you let me pay you off my debt? His name is Gil Perez. You have seen him, I know. He's an honest man, my dear, and loves you to distraction. What are you going to say to him if he asks for you?"

She stood, handfasted to the man who had kissed her—and in kissing her had drawn out her soul through her lips; who now was pleading that another man might have her dead lips. The mockery of the thing might have made a worse woman laugh horribly; but this was a woman made pure by love. She saw no mockery, no discrepancy in what he asked her. She knew he was in earnest and wished her nothing but good.

And she could see, without knowing that she saw, how much he desired to be rid of his obligation to her. Therefore, she reasoned, she would be serving him again if she agreed to what he proposed. Here—if laughing had been her mood—was matter for laughter, that when he tried to pay her off he was really getting deeper into debt. Look at it in this way. You owe a fine sum, principal and interest, to a Jew; you go to him and propose to borrow again of him in order that you may pay off the first debt and be done with it. The Jew might laugh but he would lend; and Manuela, who hoarded love, hugged to her heart the new bond she was offered. The deeper he went into debt the more she must lend him! There was pleasure in this—shrill pleasure not far off from pain; but she was a child of pleasure, and must take what she could get.

Her grave eyes, uncurtained, searched his face. "Is this what you desire me to do? Is this what you ask of me?"

"My dear," said he, "I desire your freedom. I desire to see you happy and cared for. I must go away. I must go home. I shall go more willingly if I know that I have provided for my friend."

She urged a half-hearted plea. "I am very well here, Don Osmundo. The sisters are kind to me, the work is light. I might be happy here——"

"What!" he cried, "in prison!"

"It is what I deserve," she said; but he would not hear of it.

"You are here through my blunders," he insisted. "If I hadn't left you with that scoundrel in the wood this would never have happened. And there's another thing which I must say——" He grew very serious. "I'm ashamed of myself—but I must say it." She looked at her hands in her lap, knowing what was coming.

"They said, you know, that Estéban must have thought me your lover." She sat as still as death. "Well—I was."

Not a word from her. "My dear," he went on painfully—for Eleanor Vernon's clear grey eyes were on him now, "I must tell you that I did what I had no business to do. There's a lady in England who—whom—I was carried away—I thought——" He stopped, truly shocked at what he had thought her to be. "Now that I know you, Manuela, I tell you fairly I behaved like a villain."

Her face was flung up like that of a spurred horse; she was on the point to reveal herself,—to tell him that in that act of his lay all her glory. But she stopped in time, and resumed her drooping, and her dejection. "I must serve him still—serve him always," was her burden.

"I was your lover truly," he continued, "after I knew what you had risked for me, what you had brought yourself to do for me. Not before that. Before that, I had been a thief—a brute. But after it, I loved you—and then I had your cross set in gold—and betrayed you into Don Luis' mad old hands. All this trouble is my fault—you are here through me—you must be got out through me. Gil Perez is a better man than I am ever likely to be. He loves you sincerely. He loved you before you gave yourself up. You know that, I expect..."

She knew it, of course, perfectly well, but she said nothing.

"He wouldn't wish to bustle you into marriage, or anything of the sort. He's a gentleman, is Gil Perez, and I shall see that he doesn't ask for you empty-handed. I am sure he can make you happy; and I tell you fairly that the only way I can be happy myself is to know that I have made you amends." He got up—at the end of his resources. "Let me leave his case before you. He'll plead it in his own way, you'll find. I can't help thinking that you must know what the state of his feelings is. Think of him as kindly as you can—and think of me, too, Manuela, as a man who has done you a great wrong, and wants to put himself right if he may." He held out his hand. "Good-bye, my dear. I'll see you again, I hope—or send a better man."

"Good-bye, Don Osmundo," she said, and gave him her hand. He pressed it and went away, feeling extremely satisfied with the hour's work. Eleanor Vernon's clear grey eyes smiled approvingly upon him. "Damn it all," he said to himself, "I've got that tangle out at last." He began to think of England—Somersetshire—Eleanor—partridges. "I shall get home, I hope, by the first," he said.

"He's a splendour, your *novio*, Manuelita," said Sister Chucha, and emphasised her approval with a kiss. "Fie!" she cried, "what a cold cheek! The cheek of a dead woman. And you with a *hidalgo* for your *novio*!"

# CHAPTER XIX

## THE WAR OPENS

Returning from his visit, climbing the Calle Mayor at that blankest hour of the summer day when the sun is at his fiercest, raging vertically down upon a street empty of folk, but glittering like glass and radiant with quivering air, Manvers was shot at from a distance, so far as he could judge, of thirty yards. He heard the ball go shrilling past him and then splash and flatten upon a church wall beyond. He turned quickly, but could see nothing. Not a sign of life was upon the broad way, not a curtain was lifted, not a shutter swung apart. To all intents and purposes he was upon the Castilian plains.

Unarmed though he was, he went back upon his traces down the hill, expecting at any moment that the assassin would flare out upon him and shoot him down at point-blank. He went back in all some fifty yards. There was no man in lurking that he could discover. After a few moments' irresolution—whether to stand or proceed—he decided that the sooner he was within walls the better. He turned again and walked briskly towards the Puerta del Sol.

Sixty yards or so from the great *plaza*, within sight of it, he was fired at again, and this time he was hit in the muscles of the left arm. He felt the burning sting, the shock and the aching. The welling of blood was a blessed relief. On this occasion he pushed forward, and reached his inn without further trouble. He sent for Gil Perez, who whisked off for the surgeon; by the time he brought one in Manvers was feverish, and so remained until the morning, tossing and jerking through the fervent night, with his arm stiff from shoulder to finger-points.

"That a dam thief, sir, 'e count on you never looka back," said Gil Perez, nodding grimly. "Capitan Rodney, 'e all the same as you. Walka 'is blessed way, never taka no notice of anybody. See 'im at Sevastopol do lika that all the time. So then this assassin 'e creep after you lika one o'clock up Calle Mayor, leta fly at you twice, three time, four time—so longa you let 'im. You walka backward, 'e never shoot—you see."

Manvers felt that to walk backwards would be at least as tiresome as to walk forwards and be shot at in a city which now held little for him but danger and *ennui*. Not even Manuela's fortunes could prevail against boredom. As he lay upon his hateful bed, disgust with Spain grew upon him hand over hand. He became irritable. To Gil Perez he announced his determination. This sort of thing must end.

Gil bowed and rubbed his hands. "You go 'ome, sir? Is besta place for you. Don Luis, 'e kill you for sure. You go, 'e go 'ome, esleep on 'is olda bed—too mucha satisfy." Under his breath he added, "Poor Manuela—my poor beautiful! She is tormented in vain!"

Manvers told him what had passed in the House of the Recogidas. "I spoke for you, Gil. I think she will listen to you."

Gil lifted up his head. "Every nighta, when you are asleep, sir, I estand under the wall. I toucha—I say 'Keep safa guard of Manuela, you wall.' If she 'ave me I maka 'er never sorry for it. I love 'er too much. But I think she call me dirt. I know all about 'er too much."

What he knew he kept hidden; but one day he went to the Recogidas and asked to see Sister Chucha. He was obsequious, but impassioned, full of cajolery, but not for a moment did he try to impose upon his countrywoman by any assumption of omniscience. That was reserved for his master, and was indeed a kind of compliment to his needs. Sister Chucha heard him at first with astonishment.

"Then it was for you, Gil Perez, that the gentleman came here?"

Gil nodded. "It was for me, sister. How could it be otherwise?"

"I thought that the gentleman was interested."

Gil peered closely into her face. "That gentleman is persecuted. Manuela can save him from the danger he stands in—but only through me. Sister, I love her more than life and the sky, but I am content, and she will be content, that life shall be dumb and the sky dark if that gentleman may go free. Let me speak with Manuela—you will see."

The nun was troubled. "Too many see Manuela," she said. "Only yesterday there came here a man."

"Ha!" said Gil Perez fiercely. "What manner of a man?"

"A little man," she told him, "that came in creeping, rounding his shoulders—so, and swimming with his hands. He saw Manuela, and left her trembling. She was white and grey—and very cold."

"That man," said Gil, folding his arms, "was our enemy. Let me now see Manuela."

It was more a command than an entreaty. Sister Chucha obeyed it. She went away without a word, and returned presently, leading Manuela by the hand. She brought her into the room, released her, and stood, watching and listening.

Eyes leaped to meet—Manuela was on fire, but Gil's fire ate up hers.

"Señorita, you have surrendered in vain. These men must have blood for blood. The patron lies wounded, and will die unless we save him. Señorita, you are willing, and I am willing—speak."

She regarded him steadily. "You know that I am willing, Gil Perez."

"It was Tormillo you saw yesterday?"

"Yes, Tormillo—like a toad."

"He was sent to mock you in your pain. He is a fool. We will show him a fool in his own likeness. Are you content to die?"

"You know that I am content."

He turned to the nun. "Sister Chucha, you will let this lady go. She goes out to die—I, who love her, am content that she should die. If she dies not, she returns here. If she dies, you will not ask for her."

The sister stared. "What do you mean, you two? How is she to die? When? Where?"

"She is to die under the knife of Don Luis," said Gil Perez. "And I am to lay her there."

"You, my friend! And what have you to do with Don Luis and his affairs?"

"Manuela is young," said Gil, "and loves her life. I am young, and love Manuela more than life. If I take her to Don Luis and say, 'Kill her, Señor Don Luis, and in that act kill me also,' I think he will be satisfied. I can see no other way of saving the life of Don Osmundo."

"And what do you ask me to do?" the nun asked presently.

"I ask you to give me Manuela presently for one hour or for eternity. If Don Luis rejects her, I bring her back to you here—on the word of an old Christian. If he takes her, she goes directly to God, where you would have her be. Sister Chucha," said Gil Perez finely, "I am persuaded that you will help us."

Sister Chucha looked at her hands—fat and very white hands. "You ask me to do a great deal—to incur a great danger—for a gentleman who is nothing to me."

"He is everything to Manuela," said Gil softly. "That you know."

"And you, Gil Perez—what is he to you?" This was Sister Chucha's sharpest. Gil took it with a blink.

"He is my master—that is something. He is more to Manuela. And she is everything to me. Sister, you may trust me with her."

The nun turned from him to the motionless beauty by her side.

"You, my child, what do you say to this project? Shall I let you go?"

Manuela wavered a little. She swayed about and balanced herself with her hands. But she quickly recovered.

"Sister Chucha," she said, "let me go." The soft green light from her eyes spoke for her.

# CHAPTER XX

## MEETING BY MOONLIGHT

By moonlight, in the sheeted park, four persons met to do battle for the life of Mr. Manvers, while he lay grumbling and burning in his bed, behind the curtains of it. Don Luis Ramonez was there, the first to come— tall and gaunt, with undying pride in his hollow eyes, like a spectre of rancour kept out of the grave. Behind him Tormillo came creeping, a little restless man, dogging his master's footsteps, watching for word or sign from him. These two stood by the lake in the huge empty park, still under its shroud of white moonlight.

Don Luis picked up the corner of his cloak and threw it over his left shoulder. He stalked stately up and down the arc of a circle which a stone seat defined. Tormillo sat upon the edge of the seat, his elbows on his knees, and looked at the ground. But he kept his master in the tail of his eye. Now and again, furtively, but as if he loved what he feared, he put his hand into his breast and felt the edge of his long knife.

Once indeed, when Don Luis on his sentry-march had his back to him, he drew out the blade and turned it under the moon, watching the cold light shiver and flash up along it and down. Not fleck or flaw was upon it; it showed the moon whole within its face. This pair, each absorbed in his own business, waited for the other.

Tormillo saw them coming, and marked it by rising from his seat. He peered along the edge of the water to be sure, then he went noiselessly towards them, looking back often over his shoulder at Don Luis. But his master did not seem to be aware of anyone. He stood still, looking over the gloomy lake.

Tormillo, having gone half way, waited. Gil Perez hailed him. "Is that you, Tormillo?" The muffled figure of a girl by his side gave no sign.

"It is I, Gil Perez. Be not afraid."

"If I were afraid of anything, I should not be here. I have brought Manuela of her own will."

"Good," said Tormillo. "Give her to me. We will go to Don Luis."

"Yes, you shall take her. I will remain here. Señorita, will you go with him?"

Manuela said, "I am ready."

Tormillo turned his face away, and Gil Perez with passion whispered to Manuela.

"My soul, my life, Manuela! One sign from you, and I kill him!"

he turned him her rapt face. "No
sign from me, brother—no sign from me."

"My life," sighed Gil Perez. "Soul of my soul!" She held him out her hand.

"Pray for me," she said. He snatched at her hand, knelt on his knee, stooped over it, and then, jumping up, flung himself from her.

"Take her you, Tormillo."

Tormillo took her by the hand, and they went together towards the semicircular seat, in whose centre stood Don Luis like a black statue. Soft-footed went she, swaying a little, like a gossamer caught in a light wind. Don Luis half-turned, and saluted her.

"Master," said Tormillo, "Manuela is here." As if she were a figure to be displayed he lightly threw back her veil. Manuela stood still and bowed her head to the uncovered gentleman.

"I am ready, señor Don Luis," she said. He came nearer, watching her, saying nothing.

"I killed Don Bartolomé, your son," she said, "because I feared him. He told me that he had come to kill me; but I was beforehand with him there. It is true that I loved Don Osmundo, who had been kind to me."

"You killed my son," said Don Luis, "and you loved the Englishman."

"I own the truth," she said, "and am ready to requite you. I thought to have satisfied you by giving myself up—but you have shown me that that was not enough. Now then I give you myself of my own will, if you will let Don Osmundo go free. Will you make a bargain with me? He knew nothing of Don Bartolomé, your son."

Don Luis bowed. Manuela turned her head slowly about to the still trees, to the sleeping water, to the moon in the clear sky, as if to greet the earth for the last time. For one moment her eyes fell on Gil Perez afar off—on his knees with his hands raised to heaven.

"I am ready," she said again, and bowed her head. Tormillo put into Don Luis' hands the long knife. Don Luis threw it out far into the lake. It fled like a streak of light, struck, skimmed along the surface, and sank without a splash. He went to Manuela and put his hand on her shoulder. She quivered at his touch.

"My child," said he, "I cannot touch you. You have redeemed yourself. Go now, and sin no more."

He left her and went his way, stately, along the edge of the water. He stalked past Gil Perez at his prayers as if he saw him not—as may well be the case. But Gil Perez got upon his feet as he went by and saluted him with profound respect.

Immediately afterwards he went like the wind to Manuela. He found her crying freely on the stone seat, her arms upon the back of it and her face hidden in her arms She wept with passion; her sobs were pitiful to hear. Tormillo, not at all moved, waited for Gil Perez.

"*Esa te quiere bien que te hace llorar*," he said: "She loves thee well, that makes thee weep."

"I weep not," said Gil Perez; "it is she that weeps. As for me, I praise God."

"Aha, Gil Perez," Tormillo began—then he chuckled. "For you, my friend, there's still sunlight on the wall."

Gil nodded. "I believe it." Then he looked fiercely at the other man. "Go you with God, Tormillo, and leave me with her."

Tormillo stared, spat on the ground. "No need of your 'chuck chuck' to an old dog. I go, Gil Perez. *Adios, hermano.*"

Gil Perez sat on the stone seat, and drew Manuela's head to his shoulder. She suffered him.

Inside back cover art (left side)

Inside back cover art (right side)

Milton Keynes UK
Ingram Content Group UK Ltd.
UKHW012314040624
443649UK00007B/617

9 789361 476846